The Truth Seekers Mystery Series™

The Missing Link:
Found!

By

Christina N. Gerwitz
and Felice Gerwitz

The Truth Seekers: Those dedicated to finding the truth...

John: 14:6

"Jesus said... I am the way, the truth, and the life..."

This book is dedicated to our family who made this venture possible. We'd like to thank them for all the times they listened to excerpts from this book being read and for the valuable insights they gave us. We thank the Lord who has given us faith and the ability to share the wonders of His Creation and the search for the truth about origins with our readers.

The Truth Seekers Mystery Series™

1. *The Missing Link: Found*

2. *Dinosaur Quest at Diamond Peak*

3. *Keys to the Past: Unlocked*

The Truth Seekers Mystery Series™

The Missing Link: Found!

By

Christina N. Gerwitz
and Felice Gerwitz

Media Angels,® Inc.
Fort Myers, Florida

The Missing Link: Found
Copyright © 2000, Revised 2004
by Christina N. Gerwitz and Felice Gerwitz
ISBN # 1-931941-08-4

Published by Media Angels,® Inc.
Ft. Myers, Florida 33912

Cover illustration by Home Based Publishing

Printed in the United States of America

Table of Contents

Chapter 1
The Decoy

Planting both feet securely on the deck of the swaying boat, Anna skillfully focused her 35 mm camera on the group gathered around the stern.

"I can't hold it! It's going to get away!" Christian Murphy shouted, pulling back on his deep-sea rod. The twenty-pound test line screamed off his Penn reel, as the fish dove deeper into the salty sea, bait in tow. Christian's line zigzagged in his valiant fight, prompting his father to put out a hand to help. He knew Christian wouldn't give up without a fight. With his right foot braced against the side of the boat for leverage, Christian leaned back—holding on desperately. Anna recorded every movement with her camera.

In jean shorts and a Jars of Clay T-shirt, Christian was now drenched with sweat from the tug of war with the monster fish. Anna swung around and shot pictures of her proud, petite mother who clasped her straw hat firmly over top of her dark brown hair as she shaded herself from the blazing Florida sun. Seeing Andy jump in mid-air with excitement, Anna quickly snapped her little blond-haired brother's photo. She then returned her focus to Christian as he pitted his strength against the fish and victoriously landed his catch.

Captain Slate Horne had implemented a loran, an electronic

fish finder, which sent out sonar waves to detect large schools of fish. Now stationed in the middle of a feeding frenzy, lines were dropped from the blue and red striped deep-sea Wahoo Racer and immediately hooked.

"Hurry, Dad!" Christian shouted, trying to maintain his grasp on the squirming twenty-pound red snapper.

"Okay, Son, take it easy," Dr. Murphy replied, attempting to work the hook out of the fish's mouth. A noted photographer, he smiled at the picture his sixteen-year old son made with such intense facial expressions. "Anna, I hope you're capitalizing on these photo opportunities!"

"Don't worry, Dad—I am," Anna rejoined. Taking a step back, she focused on her tall, lean father whose blond hair gleamed in the sun and showed no signs of gray. He grinned as the shutter tripped once more. "I guess I deserved that," he said, laughing.

Vacationing off the southeast coast of Florida on a popular Florida Keys island, the Murphys were enjoying another beautifully clear, hot day. They were just off Key Largo, the island closest to the bottom tip of Florida. Only two other boats were in sight. The ocean surrounded them, and land was just beyond the horizon. The blue-green water reflected the sparkling sun, and the salty sea spray offered a fragrant backdrop for what could only be described as a beautiful day.

"What an extraordinary catch, Christian!" Andy exclaimed while standing on his tiptoes and craning his neck for a better look. When the fish flopped onto his sandaled foot the blond-haired boy jumped back, causing everyone to laugh. Smiling sheepishly, Andy made more room for Christian and his father who were grappling with the energetic fish.

After snapping another shot of her family's antics, Anna lowered her camera. "This is so great!" she marveled. "I still can't believe we got this trip for free!"

A few days ago, the family had been at the right place at the right time. Having walked down to the docks one evening after dinner, they watched boats unload their catch. There they met Slate Horne, captain of the Wahoo Racer, who invited the family for a

8

complimentary ride and deep-sea fishing trip on his charter boat. It was a sales promotion. If the family enjoyed the boat trip, they would hopefully encourage others to use the charter. All that was required was the filling out of a questionnaire at the end of the trip and allowing their names to be used in advertising. After a few preliminary questions and clarifying of details, the Murphys agreed.

"I can't believe we got this free trip either. This is so cool!" Christian reiterated, echoing his sister's earlier sentiment. During his wrestling match with the snapper, his ever-present hat had fallen to the deck but was quickly retrieved by his brother. "Thanks, Andy!" Christian smiled. With his prize catch now unhooked and buried under ice for filleting at day's end, Christian felt he could relax. He baited his hook and tossed it in. "What could possibly be better than this?"

Anna wasn't quite in agreement with her brother's enthusiasm for fishing, but was enjoying time on the boat. Having tried her hand at casting, she abandoned the task upon learning they planned to actually eat the fish. She would rather stick with catching photos.

Beginning the day by photographing her family, Anna shot pictures of the boat, the scenery, and finally the crew. Dressed in faded denim shorts and T-shirt with the Wahoo Racer logo imprinted in the upper left corner, first mate Lauren intrigued Anna. She looked more like a petite sales lady than a ship hand. Similarly attired was Captain Slate, although he was weathered and wrinkled from many years in the sun. Donning the traditional captain's cap, he was busy checking crab traps from the previous day.

Taking pictures of the two crewmembers is almost impossible, Anna thought. *It seems as though they purposely turn away just as I try to take the shots. Backs of heads don't make for good pictures*, Anna huffed. She wouldn't give up easily.

As long as she could remember, Anna had loved taking pictures. Having a father who was a professional photographer as well as an archaeologist didn't hurt. Her father called her a shutterbug and encouraged her budding talent. She mostly enjoyed photographing people, and the walls of her room gave evidence to this.

A flicker in the distant sky caught Anna's attention as sun glinted off metal. An aircraft was progressively moving closer. Steadying herself against the slightly pitching vessel, she held onto the rail and squinted against the bright sky. She couldn't quite make out the type of aircraft approaching. Pushing her short, silky brown hair out of her eyes, Anna squinted into her camera and used the zoom to focus.

"Hey, look at the 'copter!" Andy announced, also noting the swiftly approaching craft.

"We all see it, Andy," Christian retorted, more interested in fishing.

"Well, I didn't know it was a helicopter," Anna emphasized, smiling to counter Christian's remark. "Can you tell what type it is?"

"No, I can't tell this far away," Andy replied, looking longingly at Anna's camera.

"I think it's some kind of government 'copter," Anna commented, adjusting her zoom before handing her camera to Christian who had now reeled in his line.

"Really?" Andy asked, "Can I look next?" He loved helicopters and made it his life's ambition to read everything he could get his hands on about aircrafts in general.

"Absolutely! Once Christian is—"

"Hey! Something huge just hit my bait!" their father shouted from the far rail.

Everyone hurried to Dr. Murphy's side, and in the excitement, Anna momentarily forgot about the helicopter. Christian handed Anna back her camera.

"My goodness! Look at the way it's taking your line, honey," exclaimed Mrs. Murphy with net in hand. She extended over the rail as much as her generous form would allow. Even though eight months pregnant, she was as active as ever.

Hanging back yet ready to help was first mate Lauren. "Y'all are doing just great," she drawled with approval.

"I'll take some pictures, Dad!" Anna exclaimed, leaning over the rail for a better look. *This is so amazing; I can't wait to get this film developed!* Anna thought.

Several pictures were captured by the time Jack Murphy hoisted a fair-sized mahi-mahi onto the deck. The shimmering bluish-green and silver fish, also known as a dolphin, was still putting up a

10

struggle. Slate pushed off from the rail where he had been lounging, watching from a distance. He hurriedly glanced over his shoulder before moving closer to help.

"Oh Jack! This is my favorite fish!" Kathy enthused. "I can't wait to have it prepared tonight!" Mrs. Murphy knew some restaurants on the Keys encouraged patrons to bring in their fresh fish and have it prepared any way they desired.

In the middle of unhooking the dolphin, everyone's attention diverted to the helicopter, as its whooshing blades grew increasingly louder. The boat began to rock precariously, and all on board struggled to remain upright.

Hastily tossing the mahi into the ice chest, Dr. Murphy forgot the barbed hook was still embedded in the fish. The trailing rod and its line entangled itself around Slate's feet and he fell with a thud. Hunkering down, Christian attempted to help Slate. Lauren beat him to it and whipped out her pocketknife. The blade flashed in the sun as she cut Slate free.

"Awesome!" Andy shouted, staring wide-eyed at the helicopter. He felt a sudden rush of excitement as it hovered overhead, making a deafening noise and rocking the boat wildly.

What in the world is going on? Christian wondered.

Anna tried to capture it all on film. *No one's ever going to believe this without pictures!* she thought to herself.

A commanding voice boomed over the loudspeaker. "This is the FBI! Prepare to be boarded!"

Dr. Murphy quickly ushered the startled family toward the stern. Huddled close, they held on to keep from falling. Bringing up the rear were Lauren and Captain Slate. Christian subconsciously held his breath as he stared up at the helicopter—and the automatic weapons being trained on them.

Chapter 2
The Chase

Ropes dropped from the helicopter and three people rappelled down in quick succession. Upon hitting the deck, they immediately unfastened their harnesses and trained automatic weapons on the unsuspecting group.

Dr. Murphy moved in front to shield his family. "What's the meaning of this?" he demanded.

No one answered. Instead, one of the agents signaled the helicopter, and it moved several hundred yards away. This helped tremendously as the boat stopped its violent pitching. Two agents circled around the deck and crouched while looking into the cabin, apparently searching for something.

Positioned before the startled group was the tallest of the three FBI agents. He looked as if he had just stepped out of an action-adventure movie with his black pants, boots, bulletproof vest, helmet, headset, binoculars, and three firearms. One firearm was in a holster while another, a rifle, was slung across his back. Unfortunately, the third firearm was pointed directly at the Murphys. Tilting his head slightly, he pressed one hand against his headset and listened intently. Eyes squinting, he looked formidably at the assembled band before turning quickly and surveying the area around the deck. "Copy. Over," he replied into the headset mouthpiece.

The Murphys gave a collective sigh of relief as the gun was holstered and a badge extracted and flipped open. "I'm commandeering this vessel! My name is Tyler Spencer. I'm an agent for the FBI," the over six foot tall muscular man stated. His authoritative tone left no room for arguing. Turning to Captain Horne, he then ordered, "Sir, escort everyone into the cabin and be seated with them."

No way! I don't want to go below, Christian thought. He exchanged looks with Anna who seemed to be thinking the same thing.

Anna, too, wanted to stay topside but shook her head no. *There's no way we can hide up here without being seen*, her eyes seemed to say.

After ushering his family below, Dr. Murphy was about to follow when Agent Spencer put out a restraining hand. "Just a minute sir; I'd like you to operate the boat," he directed.

"What's this all about?" Dr. Murphy asked. "There is no justification for the danger in which you've placed my family!" Although six feet tall, Dr. Murphy found himself looking up in order to make eye contact with the towering agent.

Spencer ignored the question and spoke intently into the headset. He appeared determined to get underway. Once directed, the other agents began pulling up the anchor.

When he didn't receive an answer, Dr. Murphy muttered angrily, "Free trip indeed!" He glared at Slate. Slate shrugged his shoulders noncommittally and followed the rest of the Murphy family into the cabin.

"I'm going to get to the bottom of this, Slate," Dr. Murphy vowed.

Halting his retreat, Slate drawled, "I'd like to know what's going on too. All I can say is there better not be any damage to my boat!" he warned.

"Come on; get moving!" the agent ordered from the deck, effectively putting an end to all conversation.

The remainder of the family filed into the cabin and down the stairs, passing Spencer. Anna heard him mumble something to Lauren as she passed by and noted Lauren's slight nod in reply. Unfortunately, Anna was unable to catch what had been said and she feared the worst. *Something more dangerous is going on than any of us suspect! Please Lord,* she silently prayed, *be with us and protect us.*

After seeing his family and the crew seated safely in the cabin, Dr. Murphy reported to the wheelhouse but hesitated to take the wheel as ordered. "I demand to know what is happening before I render my cooperation, and I refuse to have my family endangered," he reiterated.

"Sorry, sir, there's not much I'm permitted to reveal without the necessary clearance," Agent Spencer replied. Pulling off his headset, he ran a hand through his shortly cropped brown hair in frustration. "If it's any consolation, sir, your family is not what we expected to encounter upon boarding."

The headset crackled to life, and he promptly replaced it. Obviously the order was to proceed. Tyler Spencer urged Dr. Murphy to start the boat engine.

Looking through the boat's windshield, Dr. Murphy surveyed the vast blue-green sea, its beauty now lost to him. As he gunned the engine, he offered up a quick prayer for help, trusting in the Lord for His fortification.

"Follow that boat due west!" the agent shouted over the roar of the engine, pointing to a sea-craft little more than a speck in the distance moving further away.

Seated on the edge of the captain's chair, Dr. Murphy pushed the throttle forward and they jolted ahead. The water boiled behind them as the Wahoo Racer skittered across the open water in hot pursuit.

Below deck, the group remained seated and held on as they were tossed by the waves. Hushed whispers erupted between the three adults as they attempted to discuss what was happening without alarming the children. Once underway and realizing the group posed no real threat, the lone agent guarding them went topside. Anna and Christian exchanged looks, each seeming to read the others' thoughts. They were right in the middle of a full-fledged mystery!

Striving to act nonchalant, Anna grasped her camera and snapped several shots. After taking one of the fifteen-foot long cabin, she then shot a picture of the port side, which contained two little rooms facing each other. One was a bathroom, and the other contained two sets of bunk beds. Anna joined Christian and sat on a wooden bench that ran along the outer makeshift wall. Half-a-dozen basketball-sized windows allowed the bright sunlight to stream in. Off to the right, a table and chairs bolted to the floor completed the casual setting. *Must find a way for Christian and I to slip out of here!* Anna thought as she snapped, feigning interest in her surroundings.

Catching Anna's eye, Christian tipped his head in the direction of a ladder with "Emergency Exit" written in bold red words above it. The top half of the ladder disappeared into the ceiling, completely hidden from view. Anna grinned. *Perfect. If we can make it halfway up the ladder, no one will see us leave.*

Christian glanced at his mother who faced in the opposite direction. She was trying to calm an excited Andy, whose nose was pressed to the window following the chase. Speaking in hushed tones, Captain Horne and Lauren stared out a different window. Christian looked intently at his sister, nodded, and began walking toward the exit to lead the way. *We can make it, Anna; let's go!*

Quietly inching their way to the ladder, they periodically stopped to verify everyone's position. Once they were sure no one saw them, they hurriedly climbed up. Standing on the top rung, Anna peeked out of the hatch. She instinctively shot several more pictures, capturing the back of an agent, the deck, and some sky as the boat sped ahead. Following Christian, she held onto the rail while making her way to the stern of the speeding boat. As the wind whipped her silky strands of hair across her face, Anna briefly let go of the oak rail to brush them away. Just then the boat hit a wave, and Anna went airborne, landing on Christian who made a desperate grab for the rail to keep them both from falling overboard.

"Be careful," Christian hissed in her ear, "or they'll be fishing us both out of the ocean!"

Soon they were safely crouched behind the seats in the stern where minutes earlier they had been enjoying fishing. Christian looked up to see their dad and Agent Spencer above on the fly deck, their backs to them.

"As long as Dad and Agent Spencer don't look down here we won't be seen," Christian assured.

Anna nodded and looked ahead noting the helicopter was in pursuit of the other boat. *This may not have been a good idea after all,* Anna thought. With the gap between the two vessels narrowing considerably, Anna crouched and zoomed in before snapping pictures of the craft they were chasing.

"Can you believe this?" Christian asked in wonder. "We're in the middle of a high-speed chase! The 'copter is keeping his distance but that boat can't possibly outrun it! I can't imagine what those guys did!"

"Whatever it is, I don—" Anna's words were cut off by a pinging sound. Puzzled, she paused for a moment to listen. Something whizzed by her shoulders followed by another ping— only this time closer. Suddenly realization set in.

Chapter 3
Ka Boom!

Christian yanked Anna down beside him as he flattened himself on the deck. "That was a bullet! Stay down!"

"Maybe leaving the cabin wasn't such a good idea after all," Anna grimaced. Rubbing her throbbing knee, she realized the bullet that whizzed past originated from the boat they were pursuing.

One of the agents on board immediately returned fire. The dark-haired man was stationed on the starboard side with his back toward them. Another blast of gunshot could be heard from the front of the craft where the second agent was stationed. The smell of sulfur permeated their senses, as the exchange seemed to go on indefinitely.

"Look, Anna! The boats are heading back toward land," Christian exclaimed, pointing to the small palm tree dotted beach coming into view.

The Wahoo Racer hit another wave, sending a fine mist over the Murphys. Although salt water stung Anna's eyes, she used the tip of her shirt to clean her camera lens before rising up to her knees to take several more shots. *These pictures might come in handy,* she thought, forgetting the danger.

"Anna, are you crazy?" Christian hissed. "Get down!" He yanked her down beside him once again. Another bullet whizzed by hitting the fiberglass directly behind Anna. Whipping their heads around, they were aghast to see the dime-sized bullet hole.

"Whoa! That was too close! Let's get back to the cabin," Christian urged.

Anna wiped the tears away from her wind swept eyes, holding on as best she could. "We can't leave! We'll be safe as long as we stay down. Besides, Dad may need us!" she countered. Anna flattened herself on the deck as best she could, cradling her camera against her.

Torn between concern for his sister's safety and the truth of her words, Christian hesitated and watched for a chance to safely reach the hatch. *If Dad finds us on deck in the middle of a cross fire, we're going to wish we had been shot.* Christian knew he had to get Anna below deck.

After rapidly firing at the other boat, a dark-haired agent squatted down to reload. Suddenly he dropped his gun with a grunt of pain, and both hands flew up to clasp the middle of his chest. He had been shot! The speeding boat threw him off balance into a backward spiral, and he connected sharply with the deck. Without hesitation, Anna and Christian rushed to his side. Anna fell to her knees and leaned over him.

God, please don't let him die! Anna prayed silently. "Can we move him to safety?" she asked in a quivering voice.

"I'm not sure," Christian said as he bent over the agent whose eyes fluttered open before closing again. "Do you think you can move?" Christian asked, looking down at him in dismay. The agent's face twisted in pain, but he managed a nod.

The agent gasped. "It's... it's not safe for you out here! Get below deck! Leave me here. I'll manage."

"We're not leaving you!" Anna shot back, keeping her head low.

"Then help me to sit up," he urged. Christian quickly complied, taking the agent's right arm and gently lifting him into an upright position. Wincing in pain, the man managed to lean his back against the fiberglass, using the boat for support and protection. Anna lay low, grabbed a life jacket, and wedged it behind his back.

"Thanks, kids. Now stay down!" he urged.

The engine's clamor changed as the boat slowed. Although Dr. Murphy eased back on the throttle per the agent's instruction, his emotions raged within. "This is totally unacceptable! I can not believe my family has been exposed to such danger!"

"Believe me, it could not be helped, sir," Agent Spencer insisted. "Besides, your family is safely below." His tightly controlled features displayed little emotion.

"I'm grateful for that small assurance," Dr. Murphy replied, raking a hand through his hair in exasperation. Looking up, he noted a small beach in the distance with rental units and hotels lining the shore. "Now what?" he asked with resignation.

Spencer pointed to various boats dotting the ocean. "See those boats with the red and white divers down flags?" he asked without giving Dr. Murphy a chance to reply. "Keep your distance. The flags indicate scuba divers in the area," he informed.

"Thanks, but I realize that. My family dives," Dr. Murphy answered sardonically, irritated at the entire situation.

By this time the helicopter was hovering over the other boat, effectively containing it. The firing had mysteriously ceased while Jack Murphy slowly closed the distance between the boats.

"Good. Now stop," Agent Spencer directed. Dr. Murphy was very happy to comply. Rapidly pulling back on the throttle, he threw the engines in reverse to stop the boat, wanting to place as much distance as possible between the two vessels.

"Perfect. Let's keep it here," Agent Spencer commanded, listening briefly in his headset for further instructions.

Dr. Murphy eased the boat into idle, keeping it in place. He could barely make out the scurrying figures on the other boat. "Aren't we too close?" Dr. Murphy asked. His silent glaring look willed Agent Spencer to agree.

"Yes we are, but..."

Ka-boom! Ka-boom! The sonic blast of two simultaneous explosions disintegrated the boat right before their startled eyes! The helicopter immediately lifted and banked sharply to the left—barely out of range of the blast.

"What!" Dr. Murphy and Agent Spencer both exclaimed, instinctively ducking. Looking out the debris-covered windshield, they were dismayed to see the front half of the other boat destroyed!

The sky quickly filled with smoke as pieces of fiberglass and other debris began to rain down. A large wave swelled in the direction of the Wahoo Racer. Christian, Anna, and the agent huddled together and covered their heads as burned pieces of the destroyed boat showered down upon them. The helicopter roared overhead as it flew to a safe distance.

After what seemed like hours, Anna and Christian carefully stood to survey the damage.

"What do you think happened to the people onboard?" Anna asked, worried.

Christian gave her a concerned look. "It doesn't look like anyone could survive that blast!"

Turning to help the wounded agent as he attempted to stand, Christian urged him to lean on him. "I can't make it. Let me sit here," the man insisted. Christian helped make him comfortable before going to get help.

Anna uncovered her camera that had been safely concealed in her shirt and began to take pictures of the damage. "This is unbelievable!"

"Careful Anna! Don't let them see what you're doing or they'll confiscate your camera," Christian hissed as he walked by, nodding his head to the wincing agent who was in too much pain to notice.

Startled, Anna quickly slipped the camera under the oversized button-down cotton shirt covering her bathing suit. "Good thinking, Christian!"

"Christian! Anna! I was so worried!" Mrs. Murphy admonished as she made her way on deck. "Are you two all right?"

Before either could answer, Captain Horne and Lauren hurried past. Lauren checked on the injured agent while Captain Horne assessed the damage to the boat. "Who's gonna pay for this!" he began to argue with Agent Spencer.

Dr. Murphy, wanting no part of the dispute, ushered his family below deck. "There's no need for us to be part of that mayhem. We'll let the experts handle this—and we'll discuss your behavior later," he added to Christian and Anna

"Yes, Dad," they said in unison, exchanging disheartened glances that he had noticed their whereabouts.

Christian, Anna, and Andy now sat below with faces straining out of the opened windows in search of would-be survivors. Both Dr. and Mrs. Murphy sat with clasped hands and closed eyes. *I'm sure they're praying for those involved in the accident*, Anna thought as she silently offered up a prayer of her own.

"You know, Anna, we were pretty lucky," Christian commented once he observed his sister had completed her prayer.

"It wasn't luck," Anna answered, nodding toward her parents as they prayed. "We were protected by God's providence!"

"You're right about that," Christian agreed.

Back at the dock, TV cameras, several ambulances, a fire truck, and police cars with flashing lights greeted the Murphys.

"Awesome!" Andy pointed. "Hey, do you think we'll be on TV?"

Chapter 4
The Unexpected Call

Later at the hotel, the exhausted family members relayed mixed reactions.

"We're heroes!" Andy flounced up and down on the couch. "Can you believe it?" he asked, standing up again.

"Yes, unwilling heroes by way of mistaken identity," Mrs. Murphy quipped, waving her hands for emphasis. Her Italian heritage became evident when she was agitated.

"Several valuable lessons may be gleaned from this experience," Dr. Murphy began. "The first one being when something looks too good to be true—it probably is!"

Anna and Christian exchanged looks knowing they were in for a long discussion. They made themselves as comfortable as possible on the cushiony hotel couch. Their father's German-Irish descent guaranteed his tenacity in covering a topic well.

"How were we supposed to know a free fishing trip would turn out to be just a little more than that?" Christian asked, smiling.

"Just a little more?" Mrs. Murphy gasped. "We were hijacked by a helicopter-hit-squad, shot at, and involved in a chase. We were witnesses to a boat explosion, mistaken for criminals, and if that's not bad enough, we were tricked into it all!"

"Yeah, it was fantastic!" agreed Andy.

"Son, that's not what your mother meant," Dr. Murphy admonished, and then held up his hand to stop the flow of comments.

"Think about the people who died in the explosion!" Mrs. Murphy chastised. Her children immediately became sober as she continued. "What if that had been our boat?"

Dr. Murphy picked up on the thread. "Let's bow our heads for a prayer of thanksgiving to the Lord."

They did as directed while their father prayed. When finished, Dr. Murphy addressed his children. "We were involved in a very serious situation, and while it may seem like an adventure to you three, we could all have been seriously injured—or worse."

Andy came and wedged himself between Christian and Anna on the couch. After placing a reassuring arm around his shoulders, Anna listened as her father continued.

"We are currently under suspicion of being involved in a notorious act, although the authorities realize there is no evidence to link us to Captain Horne and Lauren."

"You don't really think they suspect us!" Mrs. Murphy gasped in shock.

"I'm hard pressed to believe the FBI imagines we're part of a crime ring, yet having said that, they instructed me not to leave the country! Apparently the Wahoo Racer was used as a decoy, and we happened to be onboard."

"It's not a crime to accept a free fishing trip," Mrs. Murphy insisted.

"No it's not. However, either the authorities don't know or they refuse to disclose the real reason we were duped into this venture. Right now we're guilty by association, and any evidence in our favor was blown up with that boat we were chasing. Thankfully, there was no hint of criminal activity on Captain Slate's craft."

Dr. Murphy shifted his attention to look sternly at Christian and Anna. "You're both aware, I'm sure, that you endangered your lives by going up on deck—to say nothing of unnecessarily worrying your mother. Would either of you care to venture an explanation for this careless behavior?"

Christian was the first to apologize. "I'm sorry, Dad. We shouldn't have done it. We thought we might be of some help."

"And we were, Dad!" Anna exclaimed. "We helped the agent that was shot. But I apologize to you both," she quickly added, "We shouldn't have left the cabin."

"I guess we didn't realize the danger of the situation," Christian reiterated. "We obviously didn't realize they'd be shooting at each other!" *And had no idea they'd be shooting at us, either*, he added silently.

"How odd that gun packing FBI agents would do more than decorate their uniforms with weapons," their mother sarcastically replied. "Did you really believe they would hesitate to discharge said weapons if the occasion arose?"

Oh no! We're in big trouble when mom resorts to sarcasm. Anna desperately wanted to glance at Christian, but knew better. She wondered if he shared her thoughts.

Dr. Murphy was about to speak when the ringing of his cell phone diverted his attention. Relieved for the momentary interruption, Christian sank back onto the couch, shoulders hunched over. Even though he knew his father's strictness was a sign of love, Christian bemoaned the punishment for their careless decision.

Dr. Murphy punched the talk key and answered. "Hello? Yes. Speaking. No, I haven't checked my e-mail. Yes, I will." Dr. Murphy motioned to the laptop computer sitting on the table. Placing his finger over the mouthpiece he said, "Christian, check to see if we've received an e-mail from Uncle Mike."

Christian jumped up; glad for the diversion. Dr. Murphy returned to his phone conversation. "I'll be there tomorrow at the latest. Please keep me posted…yes, good-bye."

As soon as he hung up he was immediately bombarded with questions.

"Is everything okay?"

"We're going to have to leave?"

"Is something wrong with your brother?"

"It seems Mike has been hospitalized; he's in intensive care," Dr. Murphy shared as he walked over to his computer. Christian had just completed typing in the password and hit the button to log on. Within seconds a computerized voice greeted them with "Welcome. You've got mail."

Christian soon pulled up a list of e-mails. "Here it is!" he exclaimed, clicking on Uncle Mike's screen name and opening the file.

Dr. Murphy leaned over Christian's shoulder and read out loud.

"Hi, Jack. Hate to bother you in the middle of your vacation. I know you promised to come at some point to photograph the dig, but I need you sooner. You're aware I started this excavation four weeks ago along the banks of the Peace River in Arcadia. (Remember? That's where the Mammoth bones were found in '95.) We've found so many amazing fossilized specimens—a few you have to see to believe! (Sorry! You know how I can get carried away!) The problem is I've contracted a bad case of the flu and need you here now— not only to oversee the dig, but to keep an eye on David. He has me worried. I know a 16-year old can be self-sufficient, but that is not the main reason I need you. Jim Johnson, a paleoanthropologist and old student of mine, is here helping me along with a local we hired. I don't trust anyone, especially because of what we're uncovering. Can't talk now. It's imperative you come—vital in fact, to the entire scientific community!

Thanks, Mike"

Once his dad finished reading, Christian scrolled to the top to see when it was transmitted. "He sent this at 9:43 P.M. last night."

"But Mike knows I've given up that line of work," Jack muttered, more to himself than to the family.

"Well, Dr. Murphy, since you have a doctorate in archaeology, maybe it's time to put that name back to work," his wife, Kathy offered.

"I've done my time and spent months—even years—in exotic places consumed in my work before we married and began our family. With my current photographer job I can still travel the world and bring along some, or even all of you," Jack explained, as if speaking aloud was helping him sort through his thoughts. He had a faraway look in his eyes.

"It's okay," Kathy encouraged, placing a gentle hand on his sleeve. She knew he was a talented archaeologist and yearned to help his brother. "I'll be fine. I'm not due for another month and Andy's a great help. Besides, most of our family lives close by, so if a need arose I'd have plenty of people to call."

"Does that mean Christian and I can go, Dad?" Anna asked, afraid of a negative answer in light of their recent escapade.

"Yes, if your mom doesn't need your help."

Kathy smiled at the two, nodding in agreement. "Yes, they can go."

Christian and Anna beamed at each other. *Yes!* Christian silently cheered. After a moment of silence, everybody erupted into an avalanche of questions. Each had something different to ask.

"Hold it!" Dr. Murphy bellowed as he held his hand up to quiet everyone. He looked at Anna and Christian. "Due to a lack of time, I'm afraid we'll have to end our earlier discussion. I know you both realize your lack of good judgment and are repentant for the worry you caused. I expect you to keep me informed of your whereabouts from now on, understood?" Christian and Anna both nodded in agreement. "Well, let's all begin packing up for home. We leave first thing after church tomorrow morning."

Chapter 5
On the Road

Late the next day, Dr. Murphy, Christian, and Anna waved goodbye to Mrs. Murphy and Andy who watched from the front door of their home. Although reluctant to leave, Dr. Murphy knew they would be traveling only another hour and a half north to Arcadia. Besides, arrangements had been made for Kathy's mom to visit within the week, and Andy was thrilled upon returning home to find an invitation to attend Bible camp. Everything was set.

They had packed the trailer with all the necessary equipment in record time. As a freelance photographer, Dr. Murphy was used to hauling extra gear. Being homeschooled and having flexible schedules afforded Christian and Anna the opportunity to accompany him on various trips. Anna, like Dr. Murphy, loved photography and even the tedious job of organizing and setting up the equipment. Christian preferred working with high-tech equipment although his real interest was in all branches of anthropology like his Uncle Mike. Before leaving, a quick call was made to the hospital only to reveal the fact that Mike was still seriously ill. Inability to talk with his brother frustrated Dr. Murphy; he had many unanswered questions.

Once on the road, Anna sat comfortably in the front seat of the Suburban® and skimmed through the contents of a large envelope

31

detailing the dig site. Glancing sideways and seeing her father deep in thought, she asked, "What are you thinking, Dad?"

"What? Oh, I was thinking how I not only planned to shoot pictures of your Uncle Mike's dig, but wanted to find a Christian magazine that'd be interested in them. Now, however, I'm not so sure. There is something about his email that has me concerned," he explained.

"Dad, in the e-mail attachment Uncle Mike listed some of the items they uncovered—mostly fossilized specimens of bones or teeth. Doesn't that make this a paleontological dig rather than archaeological?" Anna quizzed.

"Yes, it does," Dr. Murphy replied. "That's why I was puzzled when he brought in a paleoanthropologist rather than a paleontologist, especially if he's excavating animal bones." Dr. Murphy kept his eyes focused on the long, flat road stretching out before him.

"It says here that he has currently excavated a mastodon tooth, a mammoth tusk, and the leg bone of a Bison," Anna added. "What a combination!"

Dr. Murphy sighed and raked one hand through his blonde, short-cropped hair. "Yes, in past conversations with Uncle Mike, he mentioned many of the finds only being unrelated animal fragments— that is, until whatever it is he's just found!"

"I can't wait to see!" Anna exclaimed. She quickly sobered when she saw her father's concerned look. "I'm worried about Uncle Mike, too, Dad, but I'm sure it's just the flu," she consoled. "He'll be okay in no time! Of all the places he's traveled and all the exotic germs he's been exposed to, getting sick in Florida seems the least likely threat to his life!"

"I guess you're right, sweetie. I'm just sorry we had to cut our vacation short. I don't like leaving your mother at this stage of her pregnancy, either."

"Mom will be fine," Anna reminded. "I think she was relieved to have some quiet time at home to get ready for the baby."

At 5:00 they stopped for a quick bite at a fast food restaurant before continuing on their trip. Using the fold-down drink tray as a laptop table, Christian skimmed multiple pages strewn over the bench seat, glancing frequently between them and his computer screen. He had rigged a cell phone to his computer in order to surf the Internet. Concentrating deeply, he occasionally tapped the small touch-pad mouse to download newspaper articles and reports related to past fossil finds in Arcadia.

"Hey! I found an incredible article."

"About the dig?" Anna asked.

"Not exactly, but it happened on the Peace River in Arcadia. Listen!"

"The aftermath of Hurricane Donna left an unusual amount of debris, but investigators have uncovered more than fallen trees and downed power lines. An alleged ring of International Smugglers had made Arcadia their home. The quiet Peace River was the perfect cover for those wanting to avoid the law. Sheriff Hanson reported investigating a call from Mr. and Mrs. Robinson whose property borders the river. Upon responding to their request to check for possible trespassers, the sheriff's deputies found more than they bargained for. An old shed, once used by the Robinsons as a boathouse on the river's edge, was discovered to not only contain shovels, axes, food supplies, and stolen goods, but also electric power unknowingly supplied by the Robinsons. More importantly, documents were found linking these items to a smuggling ring under current FBI investigation. It appeared the shed was used to hide stolen artifacts. The sheriff suspects the goods had been transported down the river to an unknown drop-off point. Our sources confirm these documents point to the involvement of Nelson Stanley, a suspected smuggler who has successfully eluded the authorities. His current whereabouts are unknown. Sheriff Hanson was quoted as saying, 'The Robinsons won't be worrying about anyone trespassing on their land again. And I want all Arcadia residents to know they can count on me and my deputies to keep our fine town safe.' Sheriff Hanson relayed that a reward by the FBI will soon be posted but had no other information to share at this time."

"Wow, a mystery!" Anna exclaimed. "I didn't know there was a hurricane that went through Arcadia. I wonder when the reward will be posted."

"Uh, Anna...this happened thirty years ago."

"Christian! Why do you always get off track?"

"It's my inquisitive nature," Christian smiled.

"What does this have to do with the dig, son?" Dr. Murphy grinned.

"Nothing, really. I was looking at an article about fossilized remains being excavated and kept going back in time looking for a beginning. I couldn't find one, so I typed in the keywords "Arcadia, Peace River, and Florida, and this article caught my eye."

"I wonder if they ever found what's his name... Stanley?" Anna asked, still thinking about the reward.

"I don't know, but I could research it," Christian volunteered.

"Another time, son. We should be at the campground within minutes."

"There, Dad! The sign said the campground is two miles on the right," Anna exclaimed, pointing out the window. She unconsciously raked her short brown hair out of her eyes, and her bangs fell neatly in place. Scanning the park with her chocolate brown eyes, Anna took in the surroundings with a quick glance as they pulled into the gravel driveway. *I really like this place!*

The Arcadia Campground contained several hundred acres of recreational and primitive camping. Moderately wooded sites were lined with a variety of RVs and tents. Some made their home there during the winter months for vacation, while others left their rigs year round.

Anna smiled, recalling their mother's referral of this campground as being rustic—but not without amenities. Sporting a small in-ground swimming pool, the park also contained a playground, basketball court, and miniature golf. The Snowbird Hall was the center of ice-cream socials, organized games, and activities. The Murphys rated this park among their favorites because they could rent motorized golf carts to drive around the premises.

"When are we going to the dig?" Christian queried as he leaned forward.

"Take it easy, son!" Dr. Murphy laughed, "After setting up the trailer and visiting Uncle Mike, we're making it an early night.

Tomorrow we'll set up several tents in close proximity to the excavation site in case we'd choose to spend the night."

"Didn't Uncle Mike mention the dig site could be easily reached by river?" Christian asked.

"Yes.

"Are we going to load all the photography equipment in a boat?" Christian asked.

"Yes, that's the plan."

"Aren't you worried about your equipment being damaged, Dad?" Anna asked, voicing Christian's unanswered question.

"That did occur to me, so I brought waterproof bags for the cameras," Dr. Murphy reassured. He parked the vehicle and hopped out. "I'll be right back. Get out and walk around if you'd like."

"Sure, Dad," Anna replied, stretching and breathing in the clean but humid air. She was glad to be wearing a sleeveless cotton blouse.

Christian powered off the computer, unplugged his cell phone, and returned it to the padded leather case. "Wait up, Anna. I'll go with you!" he called out.

Tucking the ends of her shirt into her khaki shorts, Anna watched as her father entered the registration office. She surveyed the area that had hardly changed since their last visit three years earlier. Glancing up, Anna noticed a slim, attractive lady rounding the corner of the pool. *Lauren!* she thought. Gasping, Anna swiveled back to the vehicle and called over her shoulder. "Christian!" When he didn't answer, Anna jogged over to him. "Did you see her? Look! It's Lauren!"

"Lauren? Where?" Christian asked, glimpsing a blonde-haired woman with shoulder-length hair walking behind the registration office.

"Come on, let's follow her!" Anna voiced excitedly.

"We can't both go," Christian cautioned. "You stay here and wait for Dad and I'll take a quick look."

"Okay," Anna relented. After the recent boat episode, they weren't taking any chances. "We can keep in touch with these," Christian added, grabbing his two-way radio from his backpack. "Remember, Dad asked us to keep these with us at all times."

"Good idea!" Anna responded, retrieving hers from the front seat. She watched as Christian made his way to the road behind the registration office and camp store, wishing she could follow. Impatiently she waited for her father. *What's taking him so long?*

Several other campers came and departed by the time Anna entered the office to see what was keeping her father. As the clanging bell announced her presence, the smell of mints mingled with wood assailed her senses. Dr. Murphy glanced behind him as he pocketed his wallet, trying unsuccessfully to conceal his exasperation at the clerk who was filling out his registration while chatting on the phone.

"Dad, I think I saw Lauren!" Anna exclaimed as she approached him at the counter.

"Here?" Dr. Murphy looked puzzled but quickly held up a cautionary finger to keep Anna from saying anything more. Getting his message, she diverted her attention to a bulletin board that sported newspaper articles about past fossil finds—including the mammoth bones Uncle Mike had mentioned.

Chewing a wad of gum, the clerk finally held her hand over the receiver and recited her monologue. "No fire arms, no alcohol, and no ground fires—it's too dry," she stated flatly. Two slips of paper were slid across the counter. One was the Murphy's campsite registration to be taped onto the windshield of their vehicle, and the other was their boat reservation.

"Thank you," Dr. Murphy replied tersely. Usually a patient man, he nearly snapped. Quickly checking the slips for accuracy, he ushered Anna out the door and the bell clanged again as it slammed shut behind them. "She must be temporary help," he muttered. "The people who own the place are usually so accommodating. Where's Christian?"

"That's what I was trying to tell you," Anna explained. "He's following the lady!"

Gazing down at his petite dark-haired daughter Jack Murphy frowned. "I thought I made myself clea—" The static clicking of the two-way radio cut off his words.

Anna grabbed her radio and answered, "Christian?"

"I lost her, Anna. She took off into the woods and I lost her

36

trail. There are hundreds of acres out there."

Deflated, Anna replied, "That's okay. We'll meet you at our site, number..."

"Fourteen," her father dryly supplied.

Anna handed the radio to her dad who quickly gave Christian directions.

"See you there," Dr. Murphy ended, handing Anna back her radio before asking, "What made you believe you saw Lauren? I think you two have an overactive imagination."

"You're probably right, Dad. I can't be sure it was her."

"Come on," Dr. Murphy said, draping an arm around Anna's shoulder. "Let's go set up camp."

Although the campground covered many acres, there were a limited number of full electric hookup sites. The father-daughter team positioned the camper near the pond and unhitched just as Christian jogged up to join them.

Having quickly connected the water supply hose and power cord, Christian brushed his hands on his jeans. "Home-away-from-home!" he announced with a flourish.

"Are we ready to visit Uncle Mike?" asked Anna.

Before Dr. Murphy could reply, a puttering golf cart with a thin young man pulled up. "Is there a Dr. Murphy here?" he asked with a quick smile.

"Yes," Dr. Murphy said, stepping forward to take the note from the young man's outstretched hand. As soon as the messenger turned to leave, Dr. Murphy opened the note. His face paled as he quickly scanned its contents.

"What's wrong, Dad?" Anna asked.

Dr. Murphy's dark blue eyes clouded. "Uncle Mike is dying."

Chapter 6
Near Death

After obtaining Mike's room number from the front desk, the Murphys entered the elevator and were quickly deposited onto the second floor where a pungent antiseptic smell greeted them.

"Room 209 is this way," Anna pointed out, reading the sign on the wall.

"Here it is," Christian announced, standing in front of a large wooden door. "Should we just go in?" he asked, hanging back nervously. *I can't stand the smell of hospitals; it makes me so uncomfortable to be here*, he thought.

Dr. Murphy held up his hand, indicating they should wait outside. Stepping up to the enormous door, he knocked softly before pushing it open. After a quick look, he nodded for them to follow.

Stiff blue curtains partially concealed the bed. Walking into the semi-darkened room, they saw tiny lights blinking on and off and a myriad of tubes running from an I.V. that was slowly dripping medication into Mike's arm. His weathered complexion starkly contrasted the crisp white hospital linen.

"Is he asleep?" Christian asked in hushed tones.

"Yes," answered a strange voice. The Murphys jumped at the unexpected sound.

"David! I didn't see you there," Dr. Murphy exclaimed, hurrying over to the corner to hug his nephew.

Towering over David, Christian shook hands and watched as Anna did the same. The greeting was stiff on all sides. David was definitely their least favorite cousin.

His straight blond hair fell onto his forehead and shielded his eyes. It resisted his attempts of trying to rake it off his forehead. "Glad you could make it," he responded, but his tone lacked any warmth.

"How is he?" Dr. Murphy asked, walking over to his brother's side and tenderly adjusting the covers.

"The doctors just drained fluid from his lungs. Why they aren't keeping him in intensive care—I don't know. Maybe its because they don't give him much time..." David paused, unable to continue.

"I'm going to find a nurse," Dr. Murphy reassured, patting his nephew on the shoulder, "I'll be right back."

The cousins soon found their way to the chairs in the corner of the room where David had been sitting when they arrived.

"David, I'm sorry..." Anna ventured a tentative hand of comfort.

He shook it off. "Yeah, well, I don't need your sympathy. I just want my dad better."

Anna and Christian exchanged looks. Even though they hadn't seen their cousin in years, he was unchanged. *David still speaks his mind no matter what the cost is to others. What a reputation!* Anna thought.

Christian tried to encourage his cousin. "You're right, you don't need our sympathy," he admitted, "but how about our prayers?" Before David had a chance to disagree, Christian launched into prayer. "Dear Lord, we ask a special blessing on Uncle Mike. While we know our lives are in your hands, we ask that you heal him. Help the doctors find a cure for the problem. We have faith that our prayers are heard because you promise where two or more are gathered in Your name, You are there with them. Therefore, we ask dear Lord that you heal Uncle Mike. In Jesus' name we pray, Amen." Anna and Christian kept their heads bowed in private meditation as they continued to silently intercede for their Uncle. David also kept his head bowed, but his tightly clenched knuckles belied his outward calm.

Dr. Murphy returned to find the children in prayer and quietly stood by his brother's bedside, saying a prayer of his own. Opening his blue eyes and looking down upon Mike's flushed face, Dr. Murphy couldn't help but think Mike looked older than his fifty years. "It's been several years since we've seen each other," Dr. Murphy shared. "This dig in Florida was going to allow us time to be together—that is, until this…" he sighed, speaking more to himself than those gathered around him. A few moments later he pulled up a seat to join the teens.

"What did you discover from the nurses, Dad?" Anna asked, leaning against her father's chair.

"They explained the doctors suspect Uncle Mike has a rare strain of pneumonia. Apparently, there are more than fifty known strains. Right now they are attempting to diagnose the particular type so they can effectively treat it. Since the antibiotic drugs aren't proving effective, the physicians believe it's not bacterial. They did a bronchoscopy, which allowed them to see inside the air passages and locate and remove some of the excess secretions. Those have been sent to the lab for analysis."

"All this means is that if your lungs continue to fill up with fluid, you drown," David said flatly, as if stating a textbook fact. Looking downward, his straight blond hair effectively hid the pain in his eyes.

"Yes," Dr. Murphy agreed, placing a hand on his back. "It inhibits respiration, but we don't know the results of the tests yet, so let's pray for the best. Right now the good news is that he's stable. That's why they released him from intensive care."

David began to pace, "Why is it taking so long to diagnose?"

"The doctors need to determine the type of virus and even then they may not be able to treat it. They obviously don't think it's contagious or they wouldn't let us visit," Dr. Murphy stated. "He needs bed rest and careful monitoring."

Rustling sheets caught their attention and David was the first to reach his father's bedside. "Dad? Dad! Can you hear me?"

Slowly Mike's eyes fluttered open. Too weak to move his head, his hands opened and closed, grasping the crisp white sheets.

41

He began coughing but the sound was a little more than a rasp as his lips tried to form words.

"Take it easy, Mike." Dr. Murphy patted his arm. "Don't try to talk."

Continuing to move his lips, Mike's voice was unintelligible.

"Dad, do you think we can give him something to drink?" Anna asked. Glancing at his bedside tray, she noticed the empty water pitcher.

"We'd better first check with the nurse," Dr. Murphy said, pushing the call button by the side of the bed.

Realizing he wasn't understood, Mike became agitated. He slowly moved his head toward his brother. In obvious anguish, he closed his eyes. When he re-opened them, he appeared to be pleading for understanding.

"Mike," Dr. Murphy enjoined, "don't try to talk. Whatever you have to say can wait." Mike continued to plead with his eyes. Dr. Murphy sighed, and ran a hand through his hair in frustration. "What if I try to guess what you're attempting to say?"

At this, Mike's expression brightened. His hands stopped pulling at the sheets but he was unable to nod his head in reply.

"Just blink your eyes once for yes, and twice for no. Agreed?" Mike blinked his eyes once.

"Do you know why you're ill?"

He blinked once.

"Are you concerned about the fossils you found?"

He blinked once.

"Is there a problem with security?"

He blinked once.

"He's worried someone is going to jump to conclusions about what he found if word gets out," David supplied.

He blinked once.

"Why don't you tell us about it, David."

David hesitated. His father blinked once.

"Excuse me, but it is now past visiting hours," a white uniformed nurse announced, bursting into the room with an air of authority. She brushed by, walked over to the call button and switched it off. "Was there something you needed?"

"Yes, we wondered if my brother could be given some water to drink. He is unable to talk, and his throat appears to be parched," Dr. Murphy informed.

"Well, after having a fiberoptic bronchioscope placed down his throat, he is apt to have soreness, and he shouldn't try talking," the nurse replied forcefully.

Dr. Murphy peered at her nametag. "Joyce, I know you've probably had a long day, but I'd really appreciate it if you would please bring my brother some water."

Warmed by his kind tone, Joyce agreed. "I'll bring him something to drink but you mustn't stay long. Normally we encourage visitors, but not after hours. We have a two-visitor limit. Besides, he needs his rest."

"Thank you, Joyce."

Nodding with lips pursed, she exited, but soon returned with the water and set it firmly down on the tray.

"Mike, are you awake?" Dr. Murphy asked in dismay as he noted his brother's blue eyes, so similar to his own, closing. "Here, take a sip of water."

Mike gradually opened his eyes with great effort and slowly sipped some water from the proffered straw.

"The questions can wait," Jack assured his older brother. "Do we have your permission to take David back with us to the campground? He can fill us in on the dig."

Mike blinked once.

Squeezing his brother's shoulder, Jack enthused, "You're going to be yourself in no time. Then we can excavate together like in the old days."

He blinked once again, and then closed his eyes. His strength was gone.

David gripped his dad's hand but there was no response. He was asleep.

"Come on, David, let's go," Dr. Murphy encouraged, placing his arm around the boy's slumped, muscular shoulders.

"I don't think I should leave. What if he needs me?"

43

"He has round the clock care. If he asks for you, they'll call. I'll alert the nurse's station as to how we may be reached." He pointed to his cell phone.

"Okay, fine," David agreed, shrugging out of the embrace. "But if anything happens to him and I'm not here, it's going to be your fault!" David dashed out before anyone could speak further.

"Let him go," Dr. Murphy told Christian, restraining his son. David needs some space."

Before heading to the elevator, the Murphys stopped at the nurse's station. Receiving the nurse's assurance that they would be notified at the slightest change gave them the confidence to leave. In sympathy, one of the nurses followed them.

"Excuse me, Mr. Murphy?"

"Yes?"

She handed him a business card with the hospital's phone number on it. "Joyce is off duty. My name is Carrie, and I'll be attending your brother this evening. Here is the direct line to the nurse's station. I'll be here until seven in the morning. You can call me anytime during the night, and I'll let you know your brother's condition."

"Thank you, Carrie, you're an angel of mercy." Taking the card in gratefulness, Dr. Murphy realized God had once again provided a sign of his ever-present love.

In the elevator, Anna glanced at her watch and was surprised at the time. "It's 9 P.M., Dad. Didn't you say you'd call Mom?"

"Yes, and I forgot! Why don't you two go down to the car and look for David. Christian, do you have keys?"

"Yes, Dad."

"Great! I'll meet you there." Unclipping his cell phone from his pocket, Dr. Murphy headed for the quiet lobby.

"I guess he doesn't want us to hear what he is going to say to Mom," Anna said, puzzled that her dad wouldn't call their mother as they drove back toward the campsite.

"More like dad would prefer that David doesn't hear him discuss Uncle Mike's condition," Christian confided, nodding toward their sullen cousin leaning dejectedly against the wall. "Come on, let's go and wait together in the car."

Chapter 7
The Find

Back at the campsite, Christian and David gathered sticks to start a fire in the stationary grill. Due to the unseasonably dry weather, no open ground fires were permitted. Anna busied herself in the camper by making coffee for her father and lemonade for everyone else.

"Dad, is all this causing you to fall behind in your work?" Anna asked, noticing her father's tense expression as he poured over his recent emails.

Dr. Murphy sighed and tiredly raked a hand through his hair. "No, that's not so much the issue, Anna. I had planned my work schedule around our vacation and also expected to make time to photograph Uncle Mike's excavation—just not this soon. What has me concerned is the gravity of the find, as I don't quite understand the significance at this point. I'm still puzzled by the e-mail your uncle sent me."

Anna nodded and placed a steaming coffee mug next to her Dad's laptop. Following his gaze, she looked out the window at the two boys sitting around the blazing fire. Christian was throwing sticks into the already large pile while David watched.

"I called Jim tonight..." Dr. Murphy initiated.

"Isn't he in charge of the excavation while Uncle Mike's

being hospitalized?" Anna interjected.

"Yes. I let Jim know David is with us; he was supposed to give him a ride home from the hospital this evening."

"Why didn't you question David on the way back here?" Anna asked.

"He's been through an ordeal. David needs our love and encouragement, not a barrage of questions."

"Don't you want to know what they've found?" Anna inquired.

"Of course I do! I'm anxious for Mike to be well enough to explain more about this mysterious artifact of his," Dr. Murphy admitted, his voice trailing off.

By the set of her father's jaw, Anna knew he was thinking about the serious nature of Mike's condition. *Uncle Mike did look horrible,* Anna admitted to herself, *but Dad is hoping for the best and I will too.*

Dr. Murphy picked up the mug and took a sip of the fragrant brew. "Mmm, delicious! Is it Irish Cream?"

"Of course," Anna smiled, "Mom packed your favorite kind!" Picking up the tray of lemonade, she headed outdoors to the boys. Anna would much rather have stayed inside than face David who rarely smiled or said anything pleasant. "Come join us when you're done, Dad," she invited.

"I won't be long, Honey," Dr. Murphy called out as his fingers raced over the keyboard, replying to another e-mail.

Outside, Anna placed the tray beside her brother on a small foldout table. "Would you care for some lemonade, David?"

"Do you have coffee? I've outgrown lemonade," he stated flatly. His blue eyes squinted defiantly.

Coffee? Give me a break, I wonder if you really want some or you're just sending me on a useless errand! Anna thought. Instead, she said sweetly, "Yes, we do. I just made some for my dad; I'll get you a cup."

"I'll take the lemonade. Thanks, sis." Christian said, winking at his sister. He knew Anna was trying hard to show Christ's love to their cousin.

46

Anna walked to the camper and soon returned with a hot mug of coffee. David accepted the cup without comment as he gazed into the fire. He didn't make a move toward drinking the hot brew.

Not even a thank you! Well, what did you expect? Certainly not gratitude. Anna kept her musings to herself. Moving back from the blaze, she poured herself a tall glass of cool lemonade. "Well, at least the fire keeps the mosquitoes away," Anna said, waving away the smoke drifting toward her as the wind shifted.

"How can you stand to live in Florida? It is so hot!" David complained. He wiped the sweat from his brow, pushing the hair off his forehead and behind his ears. "This fire isn't helping matters, either."

"I guess I should have offered you an iced coffee instead," Anna smiled, wishing she could say, *If you had shorter hair it would be much cooler.*

"We've lived in Florida all our lives, so we're used to the weather," Christian explained. "The only times it's unbearable is when the humidity is very high," he added, "Then it usually rains and cools things off for a while."

"I'm still waiting for the cooling-off part," David retorted.

"You should be used to the changes in climate, having traveled with your Dad all over the world," Christian commented. "I think that would be really cool."

"Yeah, cool. Never having a place to call home, living out of suitcases, and sleeping in tents and hotels. Really adventurous."

"I guess no one is ever truly satisfied with their life here on earth," Dr. Murphy answered quietly, coming up from behind to join them. "It's part of human nature to be discontent and want what you can't have." Cradling a mug in his hand and walking toward the remaining empty folding chair, he changed the subject. "Is there anything to go with this coffee, Anna?"

"Sure Dad," Anna said. "Want a cookie…if there's any left?"

"Of course! It wouldn't be camping without them—that is if Christian feels he can relinquish possession of the bag."

"Christian?" Anna teased, laughing.

"Okay, okay!" He passed the bag of chocolate-covered

47

marshmallow cookies—one of the few store-bought treats his family enjoyed. Dr. Murphy passed the package to David. "Here, have one; chocolate always helps to make things better!"

David took several, eating them with relish. "I think I forgot to eat dinner."

"Would you like me to fix you a sandwich?" Anna asked.

David didn't answer, but her Dad nodded his head. "That would be nice, Anna."

Anna hurried back in time to hear them discussing the excavation site. She placed several sandwiches beside David who hungrily devoured them. "These are great; thanks," he said between mouthfuls.

"You're welcome," Anna replied, giving Christian a quick glance with raised eyebrows. *So, their cousin was capable of a compliment,* she thought.

"It doesn't sound like the site is very far downstream." Dr. Murphy continued.

"No," David informed, "it is fairly close to this campsite, which makes the find more of an oddity." He wiped mayonnaise off the side of his mouth with his shirt.

"In what way?" Christian asked, resisting the urge to tell him to use the napkin Anna had provided.

"Well, the fact that no one has stumbled upon the fossil before."

"What did I miss?" Anna asked. "What fossil? An animal?"

"I guess you could say it's part animal," David conceded.

"We learned about the juvenile mammoth bones that were found in '95… but that was years ago. Are you uncovering the rest?" Anna inquired.

"No, their excavation has nothing to do with that mammoth find," Dr. Murphy interjected, "The mammoth was found on the river's edge within the grounds of this campsite."

"Isn't it amazing that mammoth bones were found near a fresh water river?" Christian enthused.

"The mammoth bones just concur with our millions-of-years findings. Everyone knows mammoths roamed the earth up to two million years ago," David informed, annoyed at having the subject changed.

"We don't agree with your 'millions of years' findings," Christian reminded him.

"Not that again!" David huffed.

"The femur was uncovered by an amateur on a fossil dig headed by the Creation Studies Institute in Ft. Lauderdale," Dr. Murphy interrupted. "You probably haven't heard of this nonprofit organization. They don't have the funds to continue excavating on an ongoing basis, so they rely on volunteers. A noted scientist, Tom DeRosa, is the president of CSI. Dr. Gary Parker, a noted lecturer and author, has also served on the staff. They have taken many families on what they call a 'Fossil Float.'"

"We attended one several years ago" Anna jumped in, "and found non-fossilized sharks' teeth and fossilized bones among other items. How do you, David, explain what we found in that fresh water river?"

David ignored the question. "Well, our fossil was also initially found by an amateur, and Dad was called by the nationally known Historic Science Museum to officially excavate. Many museums know of his work, and he receives numerous recommendations." David paused, wondering how much to say. "This recent find surpasses everything—and it goes way beyond sharks' teeth, too." He finished the last bite of his sandwich and leaned forward with an air of excitement "Are your ready for this? We've found the missing link!"

"The missing link?" Dr. Murphy puzzled. "You mean the Darwinian missing link?"

"Yes!" David went on, "Darwin said the fossils found in the future would prove his theory of evolution. The future is now! We have uncovered the fossilized remains of a fully intact skeleton that transitions from animal to human."

"But that's impossible," Dr. Murphy mumbled.

Christian broke in, "Are you saying that your father thinks he has found a form of man that predates *Homo Sapien*?"

"*Homo Sapien*?" Anna asked.

"Yeah, you know, *Homo Sapien* is the scientific name for

man," Christian replied. "So Uncle Mike thinks he has uncovered *Homo Erectus*, first walking man?" he then asked for clarification.

"Yes, we believe he is 1.5 million years old. Don't you see? The transitional form!" David triumphantly declared.

"No way," Anna said, finally deciphering the cryptic language. "That would mean that evolution is true and that man evolved from animals. We all know that God created the world as it states in Genesis, the first book in the Bible."

"No Anna, you've got it all wrong," David stated. Leaning over, he looked urgently into her eyes trying to make her understand. "Although my Dad believes God created the world, no one knows how God did it. I personally doubt there even is a God, so this fits perfectly with what I've been trying to tell my Dad all along. We evolved from a primordial soup many eons ago. The fossil we're currently unearthing is the missing link. We have proof."

He thinks he's found the missing link... Dr. Murphy pondered, deep in thought. *No wonder he brought in a paleoanthropologist.*

"Dad, tell him this can't be true! Every supposed missing link that has been discovered in the past has been shown to be false. *Neanderthal Man*, *Piltdown Man*, *Ramapithecus*, and *Australopithecus*, also known as, 'Lucy' to name a few."

"All are valid. What are you talking about?" David asked, "They're in my science book. What about yours?"

"Our books don't contain such misinformation," Christian informed looking at his father who appeared to be preoccupied. "*Neanderthal* has always been shown in artists' drawings to be totally hairy with a hunched back. He is even given a scientific name... What was it Dad?"

"*Homo Sapien Neanderthalensis*," Dr. Murphy stated.

"Oh, right *Neanderthalensis*, that's what I was looking for," said Christian.

"Yeah, I know about *Neanderthalensis*. It's a form of primitive man," David said. "It's in all the textbooks."

"Well, in a *Time* magazine article, the cover story showed a new artist's conception of *Neanderthal*. He was bald and had no body hair. Most scientists now have admitted that *Neanderthal* was fully human. There was a faulty reconstruction of the skull base and a misrepresentation of certain features of the limb bones in one of the *Neanderthal* skeletons discovered early in the twentieth century. That's why they at first thought he was the missing link. Simply put? They jumped to conclusions."

"So you say," David retorted with disbelief.

"Well, *Piltdown Man* was a deliberate hoax. Wasn't that something about two teachers filing down ape teeth?" Anna asked.

"Yes; two scientists discovered an ape jaw and filed the teeth as flat as a plate glass window, put it with a human cranium that was found farther away and then stained them to look old," Christian added.

"Well, what about Lucy? That is documented," David argued.

"Lucy was found by Donald Johanson in the 1970's and is supposed to be one of our ancestors, but the skeleton is only partially complete, some think as little as twenty percent," answered Christian.

"Other paleoanthropologists have examined the skeleton and said it is mostly Johansons' imagination. He fabricated more than half of Lucy," said Anna, glad to be able to contribute to the conversation.

"Impossible! The arm-to-leg ratio put it at the length of a transitional fossil," David cut in.

"What does arm-to-leg ratio have to do with anything?" asked Anna.

"It is the average value of the length of an arm to a leg. In humans, the ratio is 75%, Lucy's was 83.9% and an ape's is 100%... that puts it in the middle. However, Johanson later admitted that he had estimated the length of the leg since it was broken and partially crushed. He used an estimate to acquire what he called a very 'precise ratio.' The ratio is meaningless because he was only trying to make the evidence fit his preconceived idea," Dr. Murphy said.

"Dad, you're back with us," Anna said. *What is with Dad? He's acting so strange, and is never this quiet. I wonder what's wrong!* she thought.

"I'm trying to assimilate all this," Dr. Murphy said. "It has always been my brother's dream to find the missing link. I had once believed, as he does, that God created the world differently than the Bible states. He is after all, God, and He could do whatever He wanted.

51

If He chose to create us through evolution, He could. But all my research into evolution and its opposite, Creation science, along with prayer, has convinced me that God created us as stated in the Bible. Neo-Darwinism is false."

"I thought you would say that," David replied. "But we have physical scientific proof that even you, Uncle Jack, won't be able to refute!"

Chapter 8
Old Bones

"I'm exhausted," Dr. Murphy sighed, "and while this is a fascinating topic, I think we should call it a day."

"But don't you see, Uncle Jack? The Carbon 14 (^{14}C) process dates what we found to be ancient," David insisted.

"Carbon 14 dating has many problems," Dr. Murphy emphasized, wearily rubbing a hand across the back of his neck. "Explain what you mean, David."

"As you know, ^{14}C is an element in the atmosphere and is absorbed by all living things," David explained.

"And," Christian continued, "^{14}C dating, as it is known, measures the amount of radioactive elements in once living things. When a living object dies, it stops absorbing ^{14}C."

"I don't understand this. How can scientists tell how much ^{14}C is in an organism?" Anna asked.

"A physicist invented a procedure, and it has been refined over the years. ^{14}C, which is unstable, decays and eventually turns into ^{12}C, which is stable." David began. "Since the decaying process seems to occur at a constant rate, scientists measure the amounts of carbon elements still left in the objects. They then calculate how long it would take the ^{14}C to decay into ^{12}C. For years scientists have used

^{14}C to calculate the age of fossils and organic remains," he explained.

"Okay, I think I understand that. But, David, what does that have to do with your... er, ancient man?" Anna asked.

"Well, a portion of Arcadia Man, as we've named him, was ^{14}C dated to concur with our preliminary figures," David stated with pleasure.

Anna's eyebrows rose. "What do you mean, your 'preliminary figures'?"

Christian quickly jumped in to answer. "Scientists often tell the labs how old they think the fossil is before it's dated."

"What? Am I missing something? That seems like cheating to me." Anna looked at her dad for confirmation.

"No, Anna, it's true. I know from my own experience," Dr. Murphy explained, "that an archaeologist looks at many factors to determine the age of any given find. By the time the specimen is sent to the lab, the archaeologist is mainly seeking confirmation of a range of dates he has in mind." Dr. Murphy turned to his nephew. "David, why don't you tell us some of the things archaeologists use to determine the age of a site?"

"Well, the archaeologist first attempts to determine the relative chronology for a site," David explained.

"A chronology? You mean like the order or sequence of the object?" Anna asked.

"Yes, exactly," David nodded. "The relative chronology is determined by organizing the layers, or strata, exposed along with the objects found and identified in each. These specimens are sequenced as belonging to a period earlier than or later than other layers and objects. Do you see why this is called a relative chronology?" David asked before continuing. "It's a comparison of objects discovered in the various layers. After establishing a relative chronology, an archaeologist begins to establish an absolute date for the site."

"Absolute, as in absolutely positive?" asked Anna.

"Absolutes in archaeology can vary, give or take a few years," David said.

"Give or take hundreds or thousands of years," Dr. Murphy corrected.

"Well, you're right. But when you are talking about a vast amount of time, a discrepancy of only a few thousand years is not very significant," David replied.

Dr. Murphy jumped in for clarification. "To better understand the dating method used, it's important to realize that the lab tech first asks the archaeologist, who has a relative chronology of the site, what he believes is the estimated age of the fossil. Sometimes the lab's age dating techniques can have a range from thousands to millions of years. Therefore, the lab techs attempt to choose results that are closest to what the scientist has suggested."

"What's wrong with that?" David asked.

Christian poked at the dying embers with a stick. "If all of the estimated numbers are correct, there's nothing wrong. However, this technique depends on the conjecture of scientists," he explained. "They assume that the material originally in a radiocarbon sample was one hundred percent ^{14}Carbon. What if it had already begun to decay or was originally mostly ^{12}Carbon?" he asked.

David didn't answer, but looked sullen.

"Experiments have shown that ^{14}C decays to ^{12}C at different rates depending on many factors," Dr. Murphy concluded.

"Really?" Anna asked. "Like what?"

"^{14}Carbon can be altered by significant changes in temperature, the leaching in water solutions, heat, or the age of fossil materials," Christian stated.

"We also know the ratio of ^{14}C to ^{12}C hasn't been constant over time," Dr. Murphy explained. "The problem is that the ^{14}C dating method is based on the assumption that ^{14}C decays at a steady rate. That, in turn, is based upon other factors, such as the constancy of the earth's magnetic field."

"Dad's right; I've read research that 2000-year-old pottery shards indicate the earth's magnetic field was twice as strong as it is now," Christian added excitedly. "In the last hundred years scientists have measured a steady decline in the earth's magnetic field."

"Good point, Christian," Dr. Murphy enthused, smiling at his son. "You see, a stronger magnetic field would have protected the earth from the increased cosmic ray bombardment we experience today. The more cosmic rays that enter the earths' atmosphere, the more ^{14}C there is."

"I get it. The ^{14}C dates can't be accurate because the amount of ^{14}C and its rate of decay are not constant." Anna concluded.

"Right. Scientists believe that even more discrepancies occur due to the massive burning of fossil fuels in the last century," Dr. Murphy further clarified.

"Well, this specimen hasn't changed. Arcadia Man was undisturbed and well preserved. He is fossilized," David defended while stretching and trying to hide a yawn.

"We've all had a long day," Dr. Murphy conceded. "And we're not going to solve the world's problems tonight. Let's head to bed and discuss this further tomorrow."

Early the next morning Christian, Anna, and David unloaded the cargo from the Suburban.® As a sizable mound of crates, cases, and bags grew beside the boat dock, Christian checked off each item on his clipboard.

"Checking, checking and rechecking," David complained. He looked tired and rumpled in his slept-in T-shirt. He had vehemently refused an offer to wear one of Christian's.

"You should be the last to complain, David. You just woke up, and then you were on the phone," Anna said, tucking one end of her short-sleeve pink shirt into her jean shorts.

"You could sleep through anything," Christian teased, smiling as he adjusted his Marlin's cap to shade his face. "I don't think you would have heard an atomic explosion!" he added.

"Ha, very funny. Okay, so I'm a sound sleeper. Since the heat gets so intense, we always rise early to accomplish the bulk of our work before noon. It's not often I can sleep in late! As for the phone call, I checked with the hospital about my dad who appears to be doing much better."

"Hey, what great news!" Anna exclaimed.

The three continued unloading the car and had nearly all the supplies by the boat when their father returned. Dr. Murphy had left the campsite first thing in the morning to visit his brother. Coming back with fresh bagels for breakfast, he had excellent news. "It's a miracle!" he cheerfully claimed. "The test results were negative, and his cough seems better. Mike is breathing more easily, too. My goodness! What an improvement his condition is over last evening! I wasn't able to communicate much in detail with him because he is still extremely tired, but his color has improved!"

"Great." David exclaimed angrily. "Why didn't you wake me? I really wanted to see my dad."

"Believe me David, I tried," his uncle said sympathetically, placing a hand on his shoulder and giving it a reassuring squeeze, "but you were sleeping too soundly."

Anna ducked her head, trying to hide a smile and avoided looking at Christian for fear they would both burst out laughing. This did not go undetected by David.

"Okay, let's see what you've got here…" Dr. Murphy initiated, taking the clipboard from Christian. "Hey, nice shirt, son."

"Thanks, Dad," Christian grimaced. He exchanged looks with Anna.

Anna knew what he was thinking. The letters emblazoned on his navy blue T-shirt read WWJD for "What would Jesus do?" Neither she nor Christian had been very charitable toward David. "I'm so happy to hear your dad is doing much better, David," she offered, trying to make amends.

"Yeah, thanks, me too," David agreed as he helped himself to a bagel. Taking a bite he asked, "Where do you want this, Uncle Jack?" David held up a wooden crate.

Looking up from his clipboard, Jack Murphy answered, "Put it by the tents, please."

Once the equipment was double checked, they started loading the boat. Soon it was filled to capacity. Looking at the flat-bottomed twenty-foot boat, Christian asked teasingly, "Hey, Dad, did you check the weight limit?"

"You guys sure don't pack light!" David commented, as they set off down the river.

Their small boat made little wake as it puttered along. Wading

57

near one bank of the river was an egret in search of a tasty morsel. The four spotted it and enjoyed seeing other wildlife, interesting vegetation, and numerous beaches scattered along the river's edge. Snapping a variety of shots, Anna considered the Peace River to be well named, especially at this time of year. The quiet freshwater river meandered through twists and turns, exposing high banks that gave a feeling of security. Occasionally they saw sloping drop-offs of about four or five feet where erosion could easily be spotted. The water level was unusually low for June due to the lack of rainfall, making it ideal for excavating.

"Hey, remember the last time we were here looking for fossils? We found more shark's teeth than anything else!" Anna enthusiastically reminisced.

"Yeah! It was great! Let's see... we found at least three different species of shark's teeth: Great White, Sand, and Tiger Shark— all by just shoveling silt from the bottom and placing it in a screen!"

Frowning, David asked, "Were the teeth fossilized?"

"No. They were unfossilized but doesn't it seem strange to find a salt water creature's teeth in a fresh water river?" Anna asked.

"This phenomenon is truly remarkable," Christian said, agreeing. "Shark's teeth dissolve in seawater. They are preserved longer in fresh water, but the question is how long ago were the teeth deposited here? Because a shark can go through 20,000 teeth in a year," Christian added, "we would need armored footwear in order to walk on the beach if they didn't disentegrate!"

"So these teeth must have been buried quickly, or they would have dissolved, right?" Anna asked.

David's frown deepened. "If you're planning to tell me that it's because of Noah's flood, forget it. Haven't you guys ever heard of the Ice Age?"

"Yes, but the Flood seems a more likely explanation of land and sea creature's remains being found side by side," Dr. Murphy said.

David clenched his teeth and looked toward the shore, knowing the camp was right around the corner. He was ready to argue with his cousins, but his uncle was another matter.

As they rounded the bend, Christian pointed to the right, "Wow! Look over there."

"That's our dig," David announced.

Dr. Murphy threw the motor in reverse as he headed toward shore and killed the engine. Christian and David quickly jumped out and splashed into the shin-deep water in order to hoist the boat onto the small dirt beach.

"Tie it down, guys," Dr. Murphy said, as he and Anna stepped onto the shore.

Climbing the embankment, the Murphys stood in the middle of a crudely cleared circle. Amazed, Anna slowly surveyed the area. The place seemed completely deserted except for a few precariously placed crates and shovels.

To the left was the excavation. David came up from behind and rolled his eyes as he looked at their excited faces. For him, this setting was all-too-familiar. On the river's edge, the sloping bank was roped off and divided into grids. Fossilized remains could be easily seen and were partially exposed. There was a makeshift canvas canopy protecting the entire specimen from rain. A sealed bucket of plaster stood ready to construct needed casts of any bones that might be found broken and in the same strata as Arcadia Man. Since the upper torso of the partially excavated Arcadia Man was fossilized, it was extremely hard and heavy. It had been determined that plastering was unnecessary in order to transport it safely.

Toward the right, four tents were staked off near the campfire and a portable table was used for meals. A larger tent stood closer to the excavation. Emerging from a thick clump of trees beyond the excavation site came a scowling man with clipboard in hand. The man looked vaguely familiar. When he noticed the Murphys, his expression changed. "Harry! Dr. Jack is here!" Jim hollered over his shoulder as he rushed to meet them. Almost immediately, a short, stocky man in his forties ambled out of the bushes. He dropped his shovel and came forward to greet them.

Christian leaned toward Anna and whispered, "We met Jim once before, but I don't remember much about him, do you?"

"No, I don't," Anna whispered. She looked at David, but he

apparently had not heard their conversation.

Jim Johnson, a thin, scholarly man in his early thirties, had been one of Mike's star pupils at the university years before, and was now considered an expert in paleoanthropology. Upon discovering Arcadia Man, Mike had hired Jim because the digging of bones was not in Mike's field of expertise.

Jim's brown hair sported a cowlick in the back and was its usual mess. His slender, earnest face wore a harried expression as he eagerly walked up to grasp Dr. Murphy's hand. "Dr. Jack! So good to see you again!" His New England accent seemed to accentuate the words. "I'd like you to meet one of the hardest working locals you'll ever find. This is Harry Bradley."

Harry's slap on the back was a little less formal, but his southern accent warmed his words. "Hey y'all! Nice to meet you, Dr. Jack."

Dr. Murphy's smile accentuated the laugh lines around his eyes and mouth. "Hi, Jim. Harry, nice to meet you."

Jim's smile vanished immediately as he noticed Christian and Anna. "You brought your children?" His less-than-pleased attitude made them uncomfortable.

Dr. Murphy ignored his rudeness. "Oh, yes, allow me to introduce you. I think you briefly met when they were younger. This is Christian and Anna, and of course, you know David," he introduced, gesturing to each in turn.

Harry nodded in acknowledgement. "Hi, kids."

Jim was not pleased. "Ahhh... yes, just what we need; more children!"

"Children?" Christian whispered. "He makes us sound like little babies!"

"Christian! Shhh!" Anna cautioned. *We'd better be on our best behavior or we'll give him reason to think he's right*, Anna thought.

"But they're so...ah...so..." Jim seemed at a loss for words.

"Indispensable, to me," Dr. Murphy supplied, smoothly. "They're well qualified to assist me in photography and they're responsible. Most importantly, they're family."

Jim just shrugged. "Yes, I understand your tendency to

elevate your family over your work," he stated, referring to Dr. Murphy's decision to leave archaeology when he married. "By the way, how is Kathy?"

"She's well, thank you," Dr. Murphy replied, trying hard to remain civil.

"Glad to hear it. Well, there's much to be done." Taking the pen from behind his ear, Jim scribbled a few notes on his clipboard and immediately became engrossed in his work.

Clearing his throat, Harry asked, "Have you been to see Mike?"

"Yes, we were at the hospital last night and I visited early this morning, too. He seems to be doing much better," Dr. Murphy finished.

Looking surprised, Harry opened his mouth to respond, but Jim spoke before he could say anything.

"Oh what wonderful news!" Jim enthused. "I saw him early yesterday and let me tell you, he looked awful. The hospital staff called here yesterday evening saying he had taken a turn for the worse. I quickly rang the campground to see if you had arrived, and asked them to relay the message to you."

"So, that's how they tracked me down," Dr. Murphy responded, realizing for the first time how hazy his thinking had become since concern for his brother's health had taken center stage.

Harry inquired, "How's everything at the campground? You have reservations for what, a week?"

"Yes, but if you don't mind, Jim, I'd like to set up some tents here at the site, just in case we decide to stay overnight," Dr. Murphy explained.

"We really don't have ext—" Harry began.

"And we brought some extra provisions," Dr. Murphy interrupted.

Harry, quiet by nature, didn't say anything, but kicked the toe of his boot, stirring up small puffs of dirt.

"Sorry, but no. That's simply not possible!" Jim retorted, tapping his pen against his board.

"What's his problem?" Christian whispered into Anna's ear. Anna shrugged her shoulders, whispering back, "I don't know. Let's ask David about him later." *It's as if Jim doesn't want us anywhere around. I wonder why.*

"Christian, why don't you take Anna and David to unload the equipment while Jim and I discuss this matter in private." It was more an order than a request.

"Okay, Dad," Christian complied. *Man, Jim doesn't realize how he's trying Dad's patience. Doesn't he know that Uncle Mike wants him here?* He and the others turned toward the heavily laden boat.

"Need some help?" asked Harry, happy to leave the discussion to Jim.

"That would be great," David answered. "We need all the help we can get; wait until you see the boat!"

"No problem!" Harry replied as he ambled the short distance to the river.

"What equipment are you talking about?" Jim asked, eyebrows furrowed, as he watched the group walk toward the boat. "We have all the equipment you'll need."

"Yes, I'm sure you do, but remember, I'm now a photographer with connections to magazines that might be interested in pictures of this dig. I've been a photojournalist for some of my brother's other excavations, and the editors loved the pictures I took."

"We don't want any publicity yet! Didn't your brother tell you?" Without waiting for a response he continued. "The upper torso of Arcadia Man—as we've decided to name him—is fossilized and intact. We aren't attempting to move him until he's entirely excavated. We want no publicity until then!" Jim exclaimed.

"I'm still going to take photographs," Dr. Murphy insisted. "But I will refrain from publishing any photos until I have my brother's permission."

"You have to understand Jack, this could start an unwanted avalanche of publicity. Mike had a difficult time obtaining permission to excavate. Did you hear how he lucked into this job?"

Dr. Murphy's tone turned steely as he carefully chose his

words. "Mike related that amateurs stumbled upon this find, called the director of a museum, a friend of his, who in turn, called my brother, an expert scientist, to oversee the excavation," Dr. Murphy stated what he was certain Jim already knew.

"Yes, that's right. However, as you know your brother's specialty is archaeology and not paleoanthropology. This is why he brought me in to help since that is my area of study. In addition, the problem remains that this is private property, and even though it is currently vacant, we still have many state regulations with which to adhere. If we have a mob of people trespassing, our dig may be halted," Jim stressed.

"If you're worried about publicity, I assure you that is not our purpose," Dr. Murphy emphatically stated. "Would you care to explain your comment about my brother's credentials? If I recall you were a student of his, and he retains the PhD that you are still working toward, correct?

"Well, yes," Jim stated, "Of course I don't doubt Dr. Mike's credentials…"

"I'm sure you wouldn't. Now then, where should we stake the tents?" Dr. Murphy asked, his patience wearing thin.

Jim tapped his clipboard in frustration. "I think you'd be more comfortable at the campsite," he insisted.

"More than likely we will sleep in the camper the majority of the time, but if we work late, we may need to stay overnight rather than navigate the river at nightfall. As for excavating Arcadia Man, I'll work with you in any way I can." Dr. Murphy paused and motioned to the others carrying supplies from the boat. "Jim," he sighed, "I'm tired of this barrage of nonsense! Either point me to a location where we can stack our crates and stake our tents, or I'll choose my own place. Agreed?"

Jim sighed resignedly. "This way."

After the majority of crates and boxes were unloaded, Anna walked to the roped-off section of the bank. It was an almost vertical incline. *What if this is the missing link?* Anna wondered. *I can't imagine Dad having any part in this dig!*

Harry resumed his duty of sifting through layers of dirt and looking for fossils. Jim slowly made his way around, showing Dr. Murphy the site.

Huffing as he hoisted the last of the crates up the embankment, Christian turned to David and inclined his head toward Jim. "What's the matter with him?"

"Jim obviously doesn't care to have us around—to say nothing of camping here on occasion," Anna chimed in, having heard Christian's question.

"That's just Jim's personality," David said, shrugging his shoulders. He is so protective; you'd think this was his dig instead of my dad's." David lowered his voice to a whisper. "He gives me the creeps," he confided, "he's always sneaking around."

Anna nodded in agreement "I see what you mean; he's been watching us since we got here like he thinks were going to take something." Anna pulled back as much of her short hair as possible and attempted to put it into a ponytail for the day was beginning to warm up.

"It was nice of Harry to give us a hand moving the supplies," Christian commented.

"Yeah, he's a good worker—quiet, and keeps to himself," said David.

"Now that's the ideal," Christian laughed, refraining from mentioning that they had actually agreed on something. He'd try to keep peace for now.

"Tell us about the dig," Anna urged.

"What's to tell? There are the fossilized remains of Arcadia Man," David said, pointing in the general vicinity near the excavation site of the roped-off area. "This," he pointed to a large tent, "is where we put any other fossilized remains found and label where they were found in the strata."

"Such as?" Christian asked.

David grinned sheepishly. "Actually some of the same things you said you found years ago—shark's teeth and fossilized bone fragments of mammoths and mastodons which we know roamed the earth millions of years ago."

"Knowledge acquired using faulty age dating techniques,"

Christian countered.

"This dig is so fascinating!" Anna said, quickly changing the subject for the sake of peace. She snapped a few shots of the excavation site before slipping the camera around her neck.

"Well, that is if you don't believe the earth is millions of years old," David insisted.

"Which I don't," Christian answered. "I think the earth is 6,000 to perhaps 15,000 years old. Considering the present-day rate of continental erosion, it points to a young earth. Since we know the rate of erosion in the past was greater than it is today, there should be about thirty times more sediment in the ocean than there currently is for the earth to be millions of years old."

David rolled his eyes, "You are kidding right?"

"No, I'm not," Christian said, glaring at his cousin, ready to do battle. So much for the temporary truce and showing God's love!

"I believe the rates of erosion are the same and have been constant through the ages," David disagreed. "But we're not going to get into this now," he added, quickly changing the subject to the excavation and its procedures.

Both cousins interrupted from time to time with questions.

"Each fossil or bone must be clearly labeled and its exact location recorded," David explained.

"Wow! There really is a lot of paper work that goes with this," Anna exclaimed. "Why is that so important?"

"Record keeping aids in interpreting the data. Remember we discussed a relative chronology?"

When Anna shook her head in affirmation, David continued. "Right. Well this sequence, or the layers in which the objects are found, helps us determine information about the item. For example, where the object is located in the strata can determine whether it is younger or older than the object below it. Usually, the objects closest to the surface are younger, or more recent, while older objects are buried more deeply," David said.

"But what about similar objects found in different strata?" Christian asked.

"Similar objects are grouped together. When we found the

mammoth bones over there," David indicated closer to the river, "we grouped them together. Most were fossilized fragments of bone. The mastodon was found closer to the rise," David pointed closer to the tents, "and those are grouped together."

"But, what about…"

David cut Christian off, "That's enough questions for now! I've got work to do," and without warning he strode off.

Anna and Christian exchanged looks. *Didn't he realize that such grouping techniques could interfere with the accuracy of the conclusions?* Christian wondered. *Perhaps that is why he left in such a hurry. Dealing with David and his abrupt manner is not going to be easy.*

Chapter 9

Uncovered

After spending the night in their camper, the Murphys returned to the site early the next day. Not only did Dr. Murphy feel it would be better to give Jim a day to adjust, it afforded him an opportunity to visit his brother. Mike still appeared to be heavily sedated, but his vital signs were very good and the nurses felt he would be discharged by week's end.

Upon arriving, Dr. Murphy quickly set up his photography equipment and soon a second, and then third roll of exposed film was handed to Anna who stored them in a protective case.

"Well done, Anna," her father complimented as he wiped his brow and replaced the lens cap before handing her the camera. "Would you take care of my equipment while I join the others in excavating?"

"Sure Dad," Anna said, delicately wiping the camera with a soft cloth before returning it to its padded case.

"You know, while I enjoy the thrill of the unknown in a dig, I don't regret leaving its tedious and grueling work behind. There's nothing glamorous about the effort that goes into an excavation, contrary to popular belief," he said, smiling as he tapped his daughter lightly on the nose.

"Right, Dad," Anna smiled in return, "Unlike the Indiana

67

Jones myth!"

As her father joined Jim, Anna quickly gathered and stored his supplies out of direct sunlight. She then walked over to watch the excavation techniques.

Orange ropes and florescent tape in one-foot increments stretched across the nearly 225 feet of excavation site. Although the grids helped in deciphering the location of the material and bones, the dig being on a slope made grid placement and interpretation trickier than usual. The angle on which the specimen lay caused further complications as frequent hard or constant rain could wash possible important scientific data downstream. Thankfully, the Florida rainy season upon them had been unseasonably dry up to now.

Anna gazed at the ten-foot canvas canopy erected over the dig in the event of a big storm. On hands and knees underneath it were both her father and Jim. They used dustpans to catch the thin layer of dirt carefully scraped by trowels and dumped the soil into five-gallon buckets to be screened later. Because of the slanted terrain's differing levels, excavating the entire surface at once was impossible. Instead, painstaking care was taken to uncover each section one by one as they went.

Anna watched Jim use what looked like a soft-bristled paintbrush to remove dirt from around Arcadia Man. Shriveled, hard as rock, and blackened from either its surroundings or from age, it wasn't an attractive fossil to look upon. Although hollow eye sockets seemed to stare, the most notable feature was its lower jaw jutting out in typical ape fashion. Anna soon tired and joined Christian and David.

Sometime later Dr. Murphy readjusted his wide-brimmed khaki hat and looked over at the kids. At least they seemed to be getting along.

Christian, Anna, and David were discussing Arcadia Man and screening the materials contained in the five-gallon buckets. Anna lowered her camera after taking a few shots of her father and Jim working. "Is the difficulty you are having typical for excavating fossils?" she asked.

"Each dig has its own peculiarities, but this pit is especially tedious because of the slope toward the river. Dad believes much of the earth has washed away, and the fossil has actually slid down the bank. At one time the dig site may have originated up here, the area in which we are now standing." David gestured in the fossil's direction, "This is really a remarkable find for a number of reasons. See how the fossilized remains of Arcadia Man are intact?"

"Yes, that is unusual," Christian said grimly, recalling many cases of human evolution being built around fragmented bones. *No chance of piecing together bones in this case; he appears to be all there,* Christian thought.

"This is extraordinary," David added, as if reading Christian's thoughts, "because most of the pre-historic fossils found in the past are not complete." His face was alight with excitement as he went on. "I mean, you're usually lucky if you find a leg bone one place and part of the skull or a tooth in another. But this one is intact, skin and all. The fossilization turned the skin into stone, making it very hard. It must have been buried very quickly to preserve it."

"I agree about the rapid burial," Christian said. "In Florida's humid climate, flesh would decay quickly if left open to the elements—not to mention wildlife. How far along are you?"

"We are midway through our work," David expounded in a tour-guide manner. "The cranium, neck, ribs, and most of the upper torso is uncovered. Later, the entire body will be carefully analyzed as tests are run. One sample of the upper torso was sent off for dating. I already told you that the results were exactly what we estimated."

David's knowledge was considerable, which didn't surprise Anna and Christian. For all his pretense of boredom, he really appeared to enjoy the topic. "Wow, I never realized how much information anthropologists have to piece together," Anna responded.

Christian concentrated on watching the way Jim and his father carefully brushed loose limestone away from the fossil. Hoping for a chance to participate in the procedure, he took careful note of the methods for uncovering and transporting.

"Has the cranium been measured?" Christian asked.

"Yes, the cranial capacity at 700 cubic centimeters is at the extremely low end of what we consider the range for modern man. The average human has a cranium of 1200 cubic centimeters. This

69

small cranium shows the fossil is near the beginning of the evolutionary chain," David informed.

"All it proves is that the specimen has a small head," Christian retorted, exasperated that David so quickly assumed an evolutionary answer.

"What about the size of the rest of it?" Anna inquired.

"The arms are characteristically longer than a human's—just what we'd expect from a transitional form. Since we don't have the lower limbs excavated yet, we don't know anymore than that," David said. "Most primates have longer limbs than humans."

"So you believe the fossil may turn out to be a human?" Anna asked in surprise. *Maybe there is hope for David, yet*, Anna thought.

"No, I believe it is human, just—"

"Don't say it," Christian interrupted, not wanting to hear another assumption of evolutionary origin.

Anna quickly changed the topic, "I'm really surprised at how easily they are excavating it," she noted.

David decided it wasn't worth arguing the facts and decided to address Anna's remark. "The archaeologist foundation has labeled Florida the number one place for easiest mining of numerous fossil types. Didn't you know," David asked, shaking his head in disgust, "that Florida is one of the top three states for fossil excavation? I can't believe you've never gotten into this before. I mean, this area is practically in your own backyard."

Ignoring the barb, Anna asked, "Why is Florida the easiest place to dig?"

"It's because of the sand. Instead of having to chisel or hammer through rock, we just have to push away sand or mud to uncover the fossils. Some of the dirt may be solidified and you have to be careful not to brush right through something that may be an important artifact or bone near the body."

"Is that why they're having us use the screen?" Anna asked.

"Yes, after brushing away the sand, we scoop it up with a dust pan and later sift through it to make sure nothing is overlooked. That is usually my job or Harry's," David explained.

"How can you be so certain of your—what was it called?

Relative chrrr..." Anna searched for the correct word. "—Chronology?" she beamed, remembering.

"We uncovered some organic matter present in the same strata, which has also been age dated. That is a way to confirm the date estimated," David explained. "So far all the information and test results we've gathered tell us that this could very well be the find that's going to give evolution its missing link. Soon we'll have indisputable scientific proof showing the evolutionary transition from ape to man."

"Did you hear that, Dad?" Christian asked emphatically, not waiting for a response. "There's no way that thing can be a missing link! It's got to be either a human or an ape!"

Dr. Murphy, who had been deeply focused on his work, looked up sharply in the direction of the teens. It had just occurred to him that possibly his brother desired he personally lend credence to the validity of this find. If a Creationist would concur with the evidence pointing to a missing link, it would be a great boost for evolution. Dr. Murphy frowned. "I agree with Christian. Any claims at this point seem rather premature."

"But, see the long arms and short torso?" David asked, walking closer to the dig. "Arcadia Man was probably about four feet, nine inches tall; taller than an ordinary ape but not as big as a man. The facts speak for themselves!"

"I can see why Uncle Mike doesn't want any publicity," Anna commented, biting her lip and unconsciously shuddering as she gazed down at the creature frozen in time. "I mean, what if the media found out about this?"

"Good point, Anna. They'd be sure to exploit it!" Christian agreed. "Everyone from Evolutionist to Creation scientist would want to analyze Arcadia man—each ready to accept or disprove the information."

Jim glanced nervously at Dr. Murphy, knowing his stand on Creation. He decided to broach the topic anyway. "While we have sent a portion of the specimen away for ^{14}C dating, and the results appear to be promising, we will wait until we have the entire fossil removed before we invite publicity." He pushed his sunglasses back up the bridge of his nose but they slid back down unnoticed.

Dr. Murphy scowled, "There is reliable documentation showing that ^{14}C dating can be faulty."

"In some cases and by all indications the dating method appears to be correct and the evidence concludes that this is the missing link. All the remaining proof is there in the ground waiting for us to finish excavating," David said with emphasis.

Jim smiled. "Smart kid!"

Christian's sweeping glance first encompassed Anna, then his father, and finally came to rest on his cousin. He decided to plunge in. "David, I want you to think about these facts…"

"Facts or religion?" David interrupted as he sat on an overturned bucket.

Dr. Murphy and Jim paused to listen. Harry, who was screening nearby, briefly looked up from his work and shook his head—glad he wasn't part of the discussion.

Taking off his hat, Dr. Murphy wiped the sweat from his brow and was ready to intervene if the discussion got out of hand. He glanced at Jim who appeared to be intently listening to what could soon become an argument.

Aware of an audience, Christian carefully chose his words before launching into an explanation. "Ninety-five percent of all fossils found are shallow water invertebrates which are…"

"Shell fish," David interrupted. "I know what they are."

"Yes," said Christian smiling, trying to relieve some of the tension he felt. "Then you probably know 4.75 percent of the fossils found are algae and plants, and about 0.238 percent of the fossils excavated are insects and invertebrates. That leaves us with fish, amphibian, reptile, bird, and mammal fossils, which make up a whopping 0.013 percent. Are you aware that approximately 0.00125 percent of all fossils excavated are actually human bones?" Christian paused for emphasis, gesturing toward the fossilized remains. "If human evolution has been going on for millions or billions of years, we should have a great deal of fossil intermediates and human bones. That tiny percent of human bone tells you two things: one that the earth is not as old as the hypothesis of evolution claims and two, what you claim

72

as enough evidence to substantiate evolution doesn't even constitute one percent!"

"Whoa! Hold on! Where did you get all those numbers?" David asked in disbelief.

"From a lecture we heard by Creation scientist Tom DeRosa who led the fossil dig we attended years ago," Anna offered, "as well as books from Answers in Genesis and The Institute for Creation Research. Besides, Christian is a sponge and easily memorizes facts."

"I'll have to verify those numbers," David said, unimpressed with Anna's explanation.

"Another major point," Christian insisted, "is that ^{14}C results are approximate, not absolute."

"Here we go again," David exclaimed. "Didn't we have this same conversation last evening?"

Dr. Murphy couldn't have felt more proud knowing Christian didn't need help in defending something he believed in wholeheartedly.

"Christian," David asked, "Do you agree that ^{14}C is naturally absorbed in all living organisms, but stops once they die?"

"Yes, and as we talked about earlier, I would further agree that ^{14}C contains unstable radioactive elements and begins to decay at a rate that can be scientifically measured," Christian said.

"^{14}C decays at a known rate, called a half-life," David answered arrogantly.

"Yes," Christian said ignoring his cousin's tone, "and that half-life is 5,730 years."

"Well," David huffed, "if you agree with that, then what's the problem? You should realize the age dating results just confirmed our findings."

"I have a problem with ^{14}C dating because factors such as heat, leaching of water solutions, or contact with a living organism that has a different level of ^{14}C, such as some type of plant, can throw off the results." Christian took off his baseball cap and wiped the sweat from his forehead before replacing it. "Besides, even those who think it's so great know ^{14}C shouldn't be used in age dating any organic

73

material past 10,000-15,000 years."

Anna was becoming weary of the topic she felt had been sufficiently covered the night before. *I guess it would be hard to change my way of thinking if I had been brought up to believe an evolutionary view,* she thought. *Dear Heavenly Father, Anna silently prayed, please open David's heart to understand the truth of Christian's words.*

David was secretly surprised at how informed Christian seemed to be about the Creationist position. Outwardly, however, he kept his confidence. "That doesn't prove anything, especially in relation to Arcadia Man. As you can see," he concluded, gesturing toward the pit, "he is intact and not surrounded by vegetation, extreme heat, nor water." David turned and walked away.

I can't believe David could ignore the river only a few hundred feet away. At one time, this area could easily have been underwater, Christian evaluated. He tentatively glanced over at Anna who shrugged as she walked toward her brother. They watched David retreat into his tent. "Should I try follow him?" he asked.

Anna shook her head. "I don't think David is open to anything contrary to evolution. Even though what you said was true, I don't think you should try to talk to him right now. Just keep praying."

"Okay, but now a more pressing question," Christian initiated while lowering his voice. "What about this fossil?"

Anna looked over her shoulder. "Dad, we're going on a short hike, okay? Call us when you need us to sift through more debris."

Their father agreed after making sure they had their two-way radios with them. Anna motioned Christian to follow, knowing that once out of earshot they could talk freely. Not wanting their conversation overheard by Jim or Harry, they walked upstream and periodically stopped to take pictures.

"Okay, what's up?" Christian asked, knowing Anna had something on her mind other than taking a nature walk. He stopped and leaned with folded arms against a tall pine tree near the river's edge.

"I truly believe David thinks they've found a missing link, but it can't possibly be true!" Anna exclaimed. "Something's not right."

Christian took off his Florida Marlins baseball cap and ran a hand through his short hair, causing it to stand on end. "Yeah, you're right. He is sincere, but I believe sincerely wrong. They couldn't have found the missing link."

Anna seated herself on a fallen log. "Well then, we face the next question. Is this whole thing a hoax? If so, who's behind it?"

"Hmm," Christian mused aloud. "In the past when there was a hoax the specimens were incomplete. The bones thought to be transitional fossils were later found to be two different specimens—ape and human bones mixed together. Even though Dad's specialty is archaeology and not paleoanthropology, he should be able to tell if Arcadia Man is a single subject or two different specimens."

"I sure hope he can figure out the puzzle, but that's not what I meant..." Anna left her sentence unfinished as she picked up a stick to draw in the dirt.

"If you're implying that either Jim or Harry did this deliberately, those are some pretty serious allegations, Anna. And besides, how could they have done it and why would they want to falsify the results?"

"To further their cause! Wasn't Jim the one Uncle Mike talked about who was involved with the discovery in China of the prehistoric man?" Anna reminded. Christian nodded his head and she continued. "Well, that entire case for an ancient man was built around a portion of a skull and a few teeth. Of course Jim is determined for evolution to be more than simply a hypothesis!"

"Therefore, it would explain his motive, that he might go to any length to prove his hypothesis is fact!" Christian stated following Anna's train of thought.

"I guess this is sounding a little farfetched, but..."

"We better keep our eyes open. If something strange is going on, we may be able to help uncover it," Christian said, grinning. "No pun intended!" he added.

Anna laughed at her brother's remark.

Returning to the excavation site, the two teens observed their father's five-gallon bucket was full and ready to be screened.

"We can screen that," Christian offered.

"Oh, hi. I was going over to the tent to look at the artifacts.

Sure, you can sift through this pile. We're saving slivers of bone and anything else that appears to be significant. You can also sort what's in those bags," he said, indicating plastic bags containing what appeared to be bone fragments inside.

"Wow, that looks like trying to find a needle in a hay stack," Anna remarked.

"That's the tedious part of archaeology," Dr. Murphy teased, pulling on her ponytail. "Remember, it's not all Indiana Jones!"

"Right, Dad. But even if you don't try, you do look the part!" Anna said smiling. The family often teased her father by calling him Indy, especially when he wore his wide-brimmed safari hat.

"There's a lot of dirt accumulated, Dad," Christian replied, noticing the gallons of dirt waiting to be screened.

"Yes, there is. I think I'll continue to excavate, and you two work together to sift this material."

"Where are Jim and Harry, Dad?" Christian asked, noticing their absence.

"They went to get supplies. Before our arrival one of them had to stay with the dig at all times."

"Did David go, too?" Anna asked. It had become strangely quiet.

"Yes, Jim and Harry dropped David off at the hospital to visit his dad while they were in town," Dr. Murphy explained. "After they return we'll go back to the camper for the evening."

"Why Dad?" Anna asked in surprise, disappointed they wouldn't spend the night at the dig. "We stayed in the camper last night."

Dr. Murphy shook his head, "I want a quiet place where I can have a chance to contemplate this 'Arcadia Man' and do some research of my own. I'll need your help."

"You don't really think this could be the missing link?" Christian exclaimed, not certain what his father was implying.

"I don't know what to think!" Dr. Murphy exclaimed, his shoulders slumping. "Looking at the evidence currently presented, this is nothing short of an incredible discovery."

Chapter 10
The Investigation

The exhausted Murphys arrived at the camper late that afternoon. After unlocking the door, Christian immediately raided the portable refrigerator.

"Christian, it's not even dinnertime," Anna admonished before Christian shut the refrigerator door in disgust.

"Don't worry! I can't eat anything anyway, because there's nothing to eat!"

Walking over to his makeshift desk, Dr. Murphy flipped the switch to boot up his laptop. "I forgot we needed to get groceries," he absentmindedly stated over his shoulder. The flashing and beeping computer drew his attention, and soon he was clicking the mouse as the familiar electronic gurgle began the online connection. Already preoccupied with his work, he didn't look up or hear when Christian asked him a question.

"Dad," Christian repeated, this time with a bit more emphasis in his voice. "Can Anna and I please go into town to get some food?"

"Oh! Sorry." Dr. Murphy looked up, grinning sheepishly. "Yes, of course, here's some money."

"Thanks Dad," Anna replied, heading for the tiny bathroom to wash up. "I think I'll change into a clean shirt before we go. You should too, Christian."

"Come on, Anna; I'll change later. I'm starved!" Christian countered impatiently

"Suit yourself!" she replied.

When Christian saw he'd have to wait for Anna anyway, he grabbed a clean T-shirt from his bag and slipped it on. Even more than his love of wearing his baseball cap was his love of wearing T-shirts with a religious message. This one posed a question on the front, Would your hero die for you? while the back asked, Who's your hero? Smaller text underneath then declared Jesus as the hero who died for all.

"Ready?" Christian asked.

"In a minute!" came the reply. Anna returned carrying several cartons of exposed film. "Maybe we'll find a photo developing shop nearby, and I can get our vacation pictures developed."

Leaving their dad buried in his research, both teens hopped into the car. Turning east out of the campground entrance, Christian headed to town following a white mini-van. He was grateful to have gotten his driver's license the previous December, just after his sixteenth birthday. While driving along the two-lane road and taking in the quaint countryside, they were startled by a dark blue Range Rover® which raced by, cut in front of them, and narrowly missed an oncoming car in the other lane. The oncoming car blared its horn.

"Man! That guy can't drive!" Christian fumed, gripping the wheel tighter than necessary.

"We should report it to the highway patrol," Anna stated emphatically. "Someone could have been killed!"

Obviously shaken by the narrow escape, Christian didn't answer but concentrated on his driving and safely pulled into the grocery store parking lot five minutes later. Anna dropped her rolls of film off, making sure to note the day they would be ready. Within thirty minutes the two easily found the food items they needed and headed out the door.

Christian unlocked the rear cargo doors and effortlessly hoisted the bags into the car. "You could help, Anna," he teased.

"Christian! Look! Over there—across the street," Anna said

78

almost losing her grip on her shoulder bag as she tried to point.

"Yeah, it's the dark blue Range Rover® that cut us off! Hey, is that…"

"Lauren!" Anna gasped.

"You're right!" Christian agreed in disbelief.

Lauren strode down the sidewalk in front of a drug store, unaware of the Murphys staring at her. Although directly across the street and partially hidden behind the open rear doors of the Suburban,® Christian and Anna instinctively ducked.

At that moment, Harry rushed out of the drug store with a bag in hand and plowed into Lauren, scattering her packages to the ground. Flustered, he quickly bent to help Lauren and then parted in the opposite direction, nervously looking behind him.

Christian and Anna silently watched the entire interlude. "Where do you think Harry is going in such a hurry?" Anna asked.

"I don't know, but right now I'm more interested in Lauren. Get in the car; I want to follow her and find out what she's up to."

Anna stood dumbfounded as she watched her brother throw the remaining bags into the car. "Christian?"

"We don't have time to argue, Anna. Let's go!"

Anna quickly entered the car and adjusted her seat belt. "I don't believe this! Lauren is headed right for the Range Rover®!"

Hopping into the passenger seat with familiarity, Lauren threw her head back and laughed at something the young male driver said as he U-turned and quickly pulled away from the curb.

A moment later Christian put on his turn signal and carefully pulled into traffic not far behind. Being a cautious driver, he had trouble keeping up with the speeding SUV.

"What's going on?" Anna wondered aloud. "I guess I really did see Lauren at the campground!"

"Yeah, but the question is, what is she doing here?" Christian asked. "And what about Harry? What was his rush?"

"But, I liked Lauren. She was so nice on the fishing trip," Anna lamented.

"I personally think Lauren was very helpful aboard the boat, but working for Captain Horne makes her guilty by association. And

79

something seems out of place," Christian mused.

"Hmm, I wonder what she's doing here—so far from the Keys," Anna said, following Christian's train of thought.

"Not to mention her association with a reckless driver. That's two strikes against her," Christian added.

"You don't suppose she could be following us. That would explain why she was at the campground."

"That could be, but it looks like we've turned the tables on Lauren," Christian reminded his sister as he slowed for a traffic light. Still in sight, the SUV was a few lights ahead.

"Christian, maybe we should go to the sheriff," Anna pleaded, biting her bottom lip. "I mean, for all we know, Lauren could be dangerous. After all, the police did arrest her and Captain Horne after the mix-up in the Keys."

"Obviously they didn't have enough evidence to detain her for long," Christian pointed out. Before Anna could object he continued. "Look Anna, we don't have any information to give the authorities. What do we say? Umm… this suspicious lady was first mate on a fishing boat that was taken over by the FBI looking for something— what, we don't know since we aren't privy to FBI inside info. Now she's here in Arcadia. Please arrest her, officer, please?"

Anna received his sarcasm in silence, making a point to turn her head toward the window.

"Anna," Christian sighed. "Let's be practical. Personally, I wish we could call the authorities. Let's face it, we suspect her because she is here and we associate her with questionable circumstances. But truthfully? She could be on vacation. I say let's keep our eyes open and our mouths shut. We don't have any evidence—only lots of questions."

"Deal," Anna agreed with some resignation. "Maybe we can piece together the information once we learn her destination."

"Looks like we have a destination, but I don't think it's going to help," Christian admitted, pulling the car over to the curb. Ahead, the SUV veered sharply into a motel parking lot where a neon sign flashed Stay-A-Night.

"Let's leave the car here and get a closer look. That building will give us cover," Christian said pointing to a run-down building next to the motel.

"Christian, you're beginning to sound like a detective," Anna giggled nervously. Being a mystery fan herself, she couldn't suppress the desire to find out more.

"Yeah? Well this is real life!"

They hurried toward the cover of the abandoned building. Fortunately, the SUV was parked in front of the two-story motel. A door slammed on the second floor. Christian motioned for Anna to stay put as he flattened himself against the building and peeked around the corner. Before Christian could think of what to do next, he saw a curtain move, and the window opened seconds later. It was Lauren!

"It's them!" Christian hissed.

"Can you see what they're doing?" Anna urgently asked.

"No, but Lauren just opened the window and is standing there. Too bad I can't lip read."

"We can't stay here forever," Anna challenged. "We have groceries in the car!"

"Oh, thanks Anna. Foiled again, the top notch detectives are forced to leave their post because the groceries are in the car."

"Funny, Christian," Anna scolded. "But unless you have a plan, standing out here is futile."

"You're right. But wouldn't it be great to see Lauren's face if we went to the door and knocked?" Christian asked.

"Yes, and say, 'Excuse me Lauren, but what are you doing in Arcadia? We have this gut feeling that you are not a criminal, but your associates look awfully suspicious.'"

Christian played along, "And who's your friend? Please tell him that we'd consider revoking his license if we had any authority."

Anna giggled, "Come on Christian, it's time to go."

"Let's get—" Christian's words were cut off by a sudden crash and a terrifying scream coming from the second floor of the motel!

Chapter 11
The Bird Link

"What was that?" Anna gasped.

"Someone in tremendous pain!" Christian replied, looking up at the still open but now empty motel window. "What do you think we should do?" he asked.

"There is nothing we can do, Christian. Let's wait and see what happens. If we hear another scream, we'll call the sheriff." Anna kept looking behind to make sure no one would sneak up on them, taking them unaware.

"Anna, stop that!" Christian urged. "You're making me nervous."

After looking at his watch for the tenth time, Christian sighed and said, "It's been ten minutes and you're right; we'd better get back. Whoever screamed isn't doing it again." Getting back into the car, Christian surprised Anna by slowly driving past the motel.

"Christian, what are you doing! Have you lost a brain cell? Aren't you worried about being seen?" Anna huffed, horrified. "You're taking this spy thing a bit too seriously."

"Calm down, Anna. They don't know our car; besides, with our tinted windows we won't be recognized. At any rate if Lauren did see us, what is she going to say—'What are you doing here?' At least we have a legitimate reason for being in town. What's her excuse?"

"I guess you're right," Anna agreed. She breathed a silent prayer for safety and a sigh of relief when they passed the motel without event. Within minutes, they arrived at the campsite and relayed their adventure to their father.

Their Dad sighed, rubbing his tired eyes. He hadn't moved from the computer in over an hour. "I don't like the idea of you following anyone, let alone Lauren," he grimly stated. "What has gotten into you two? What mystery are you trying to solve? Hold it!" He put up his hand before either of them could speak. "I don't want to know; I'm just glad you're safe. I was so engrossed in my work I didn't notice the time, or I'd have been worried."

"Sorry, Dad. It's my fault," Christian said, assuming the blame for their behavior. "I wanted to see if I could shed some light on why Lauren might be in Arcadia."

"I admit it does appear to be more than a coincidence—almost as if she's following us. But why?" Dr. Murphy wondered.

"That's the great unknown question. It doesn't make sense that the first-mate of a fishing boat in the Keys is in Arcadia vacationing," Christian reiterated.

"Well," Dr. Murphy stated, "we're not going to figure this out tonight." Standing to stretch, he noticed the groceries for the first time. Anna began making a simple meal while Christian put away the remainder of the food before sitting across from his dad with drinks for all.

"How's your research going, Dad?" Anna asked, removing the cooked chicken from the microwave and setting it and the prepared salads on the table. She picked up the stack of disposable plates and silverware next to Christian.

"Not too well," her father replied, stacking his papers. "I've contacted a scientist on staff at the Institute for Creation Research and asked him to email me some archive information on transitional forms. I spent the remainder of my time researching articles on the missing link. I found an interesting but discouraging article written in the November '99 issue of the *National Geographic* magazine," Dr. Murphy answered, his serious blue eyes reflecting his mood. He stood to move his notes and computer to an empty shelf in order to make room for their meal.

"What did it say?" Christian questioned. He reached over his empty plate to the salad, plopped a huge piece of lettuce leaf into his mouth, and hungrily munched away.

"Let's say grace, shall we?" Dr. Murphy asked pointedly, sitting down to join them and frowning at his son's table manners.

They all bowed their heads and prayed together. "Bless us Oh Lord and these thy gifts, which we are about to receive from thy bounty, through Christ our Lord." When a chorus of "Amen" rang out, Dr. Murphy added, "And please guide us, Lord, into the knowledge of the truth."

After the food was passed around, Dr. Murphy began to explain what he found. "The article I read focuses on a startling discovery. It appears that a missing link of sorts, or rather a transitional fossil between a dinosaur and bird, was excavated. Most paleontologists today believe birds evolved from dinosaurs."

"What?" Anna stopped chewing as she looked at her father in disbelief.

"Maybe you should read us the article, Dad," Christian replied. His face looked equally annoyed as he set his fork down in order to give the matter his undivided attention. "It sounds more like a fairy tale!"

"First, let me give you a little background," Dr. Murphy explained. "Fossilized remains of birds are rare because their bones are small, hollow, and delicate. Because of their soft feathers, you will find few preserved. The fossil of the oldest known bird is the Archaeopteryx, which was first discovered in Germany in 1861 and considered the missing link between reptiles and birds because it had teeth and claws.

"Of course we don't believe that!" Anna exclaimed.

"Did they find another one of these birds recently?" Christian asked.

"Perhaps. What they discovered is a fossil in an area known as the Liaoning Province, in China. The dinosaur-bird is called *Archaeoraptor*, and it was preserved because of the area's fine lake sediments and volcanic ash. This sediment preserved the soft tissue and feathers of the bird. *Archaeoraptor* demonstrates a stage not represented by any other dinosaur. The relationship of its shoulder girdle to its front arms are sophisticated enough to suggest it may have been able to fly."

"How old do they think it is?" Christian asked.

"120 million years."

"Let me guess—using faulty age-dating!" Christian commented.

"I don't know. The article doesn't say what they used to age date it," Dr. Murphy admitted as he brought his laptop down to the table. "Here, let me read it to you:

Two fossil species with distinctive feather imprints and dinosaur features were recently unveiled by a fossil dealer. Ji Qiang, a paleontologist, expressed great excitement over this specimen. The discovery, he argued, provides the first real evidence that dinosaurs gave rise to birds."

"What else does it say?" Christian mumbled with a mouth full of chicken.

Dr. Murphy exchanged looks with Christian and Anna before continuing. "It further states:

The discovery was hailed as the best evidence to date for Darwin's so-called missing link. Paleontolgists in China unearthed the fossil of a half-bird, half-dinosaur in 1996."

Looking up from the computer screen, he saw that both Christian and Anna had stopped eating.

"Dad, that can't be true—can it?" Anna asked.

"As unlikely as it appears, I can't say for sure. I know there are some basic differences in the anatomical structure of birds and dinosaurs, but I don't know the specifics; I wish I had retained what I learned in my biology classes. If it's true, this find is said to have irrefutable evidence of a transitional form between one major kind and another. According to this article, the long sought after evidence has finally been found." A moment later he added, "And maybe not just in China but here as well."

"Where did you say this article was published?" Anna asked.

"*National Geographic.*"

"Oh." Anna's face registered defeat as she heard the name of the well-known journal of science and history.

"There's got to be a rational explanation," Christian retorted.

"I wish there were, but the article appears pretty damaging. I'm not going to believe it without further research, but it wasn't published in some rag magazine used as a liner for a pet cage," Dr. Murphy said shaking his head. "You know, there's one thing I've been mulling over all afternoon."

"What's that, Dad?" Anna asked.

"It's a comment David made. He stated that Mike believed in God but also considered evolution a valid theory. Yet, David has taken his Dad's beliefs one-step further and excluded God. I've seen this happen repeatedly. When truth must be validated by scientific standards, faith tends to decay."

"And with a preconceived mindset," Christian concluded, "it's easy for David to interpret the evidence he sees as supporting the evolutionary belief that all living things evolved from a simple beginning over millions of years."

"That doesn't leave much room for God," Anna glumly added.

The Murphys ate their dinner in silence, each deep in their own thoughts.

"So what are you going to do about the article, Dad?" Anna finally asked, pushing her empty plate away and resting her chin on folded hands.

"After reading an article like this, even though it's presented as fact, I'm not going to jump to any conclusions. At least I'll try not to! I am going to pray, think, and research further before I decide whether or not it holds any validity." Dr. Murphy rose, taking his paper plate to the trash bin. "Thanks, kids. That was a good meal! I think I'll go visit Mike at the hospital," he tried to say light heartedly, but his tone faltered.

"Do you mind if we stay here?" Anna asked.

"Actually, I'd prefer it. I'm hoping to speak to Mike in detail about the dig."

"And I'm going to do some further research on the

mysterious case that happened here in Arcadia," Christian informed. "I want to see if the authorities ever found Nelson Stanley."

Dr. Murphy shook his head at Christian's fascination with the artifacts mystery that took place thirty years ago. "That's fine, Son, but I'd like to leave for the dig early tomorrow morning. It's already Tuesday and we know very little about the problems plaguing your Uncle. If Mike is well, I plan to spend several nights at the site. You two might want to pack a few changes of clothing."

Dr. Murphy left after putting some of his own things into a backpack in case the kids were in bed when he returned. After showering, Anna called it a night. Christian soon followed, but not before discovering through his research that the old Arcadian artifact mystery had never been solved—nor had Nelson Stanley ever been caught!

Chapter 12

Passage of No Return

Anna couldn't believe it was only Thursday. It seemed like several weeks since they had left the Keys, when in reality just four days had passed. The previous day had been spent sifting through what seemed like tons of debris at the dig to find bits of fossilized remains. It had been a discouraging day. The yield for all their screening efforts was barely a baggie full of fossilized fragments waiting to be identified. Also, Dr. Murphy had been downcast since his visit with Uncle Mike earlier in the week revealed little. Still recovering from pneumonia, Mike wasn't strong enough to carry on a conversation.

At least dad's email from the staff member of the Institute for Creation Research was favorable, Anna thought. The response in answer to her father's question stated that the fossil record had yet to reveal any transitional forms that had been positively validated. What great news for dad since it confirms what he suspected!

Anna poked her head into Christian and David's tent. "Rise and shine!" she cheerful announced.

"Umph!" Christian rolled over pretending not to hear.

"Come on! Wake up. We haven't got all day!"

"Okay, okay. You win."

"Breakfast is ready—everyone else has already eaten and

are at work. Oh, and make sure you wake up Sleepy Head number two. We have a long day of canoeing ahead of us," Anna reminded. She bounded out of the boy's tent and ducked into hers bent on retrieving a hair band. *I'm so excited Dad finally gave us permission to explore the Peace River!*

"Anna," Christian called, waiting for her to poke her head back into his tent.

"No, I don't do room service," she stated. She tried to look stern but her laughing eyes gave her away.

"Okay, okay... Hey, wait a minute. Could you get me a cup of water?"

"Water?" Anna said puzzled. "I already told you—"

"No, not to drink."

"Christian!" Anna cried out with a laugh, realizing what he had in mind.

"You know how difficult it is to wake David. I've already tried. Besides, I doubt he slept well as he tossed and turned half the night. If you want to get going anytime soon, I promise this will work. A little cold water on his face, and he'll be up in a flash."

Anna wrinkled her nose at Christian, and then squatted at the entrance of the tent. Observing the still sleeping form of David, she gingerly poked him. "David! Wake up!" When she didn't get a response, she began to shake his leg in earnest. "Come on, wake up!" All her prodding was to no avail. He didn't budge an inch. "Oh, well," she shrugged, "he can't blame me; I tried!"

Returning with the water, she gave Christian the honor. He promptly dowsed David's face.

David shot up and groggily looked around. "You! You!" he spurted, stabbing the air with his index finger. His disarrayed hair was standing on end.

Christian and Anna looked at each other then burst out laughing. They were laughing so hard that Christian's stomach began to ache and Anna's eyes watered. "We tried to wake you, David! Believe me, this was the last resort!" Anna said, still chuckling.

Still flushed from his deep sleep, David's face turned into a scowl. "Laugh now, but I'll get my revenge!"

David jumped on Christian and soon the boys were falling over each other trying to get out of the tangle of sleeping bags. Anna stepped out of the way just in time as the boys stumbled out of the tent. Christian continued laughing as he ran away from David. Three inches taller and twenty pounds lighter, Christian quickly out distanced his cousin.

Huffing, David came back to the clearing where he found Anna packing up the gear for the canoe trip. He sat on a makeshift bench and raked both hands through his hair. "Christian's got another thing coming if he thinks he can get away so easily," he fumed.

"Oh, David," Anna encouraged, "Christian was just playing around. We wanted to get this canoe trip underway."

Christian came back into the clearing. *I guess David's given up,* he thought, watching as his cousin sat down. David, however, hadn't cooled down so easily. As soon as Christian was in sight, David jumped up and charged after him.

"Ahhh! I'll get you yet," he yelled, sprinting after Christian.

Christian did an about face and earnestly began running. Looking over his shoulder to see David gaining on him, he changed course and headed for the river. Not losing a stride, Christian jumped feet first off the six-foot drop into the soft sand and proceeded to splash into the tea colored water. David skidded to a halt.

"Come on in, David, the water's great! Refreshing, too," Christian teased.

For the first time David really smiled. Why not? Without further hesitation he jumped in, as well. "Geronimo!" he bellowed, "Look out below!" Soon the boys were thoroughly soaked. David sputtered, "You can run, but you can't hide!"

Christian laughingly replied, "Who wants to hide?"

Moments later, Anna persuaded the two drenched boys to get out and help pack for their canoe trip. "You know alligators live in this river," Anna warned. *Although I haven't seen any,* she thought to herself. She knew that alligators could be found in most fresh water rivers and lakes in Florida. The ploy worked.

Christian glanced around uneasily. "This murky water would be a perfect cover. Okay, I'm getting out." While heading toward shore, Christian glanced nervously over his shoulder only to see a big hump heading his way. It grabbed one of his ankles. "Let go!" Kicking with all his might, Christian pulled away in terror.

Just then David surfaced. "Ugghh!" he yelled, grabbing his throbbing forehead.

Christian was visibly upset and gave David a stormy glare.

For a brief moment Anna was afraid he would physically harm David again. "Christian, calm down!"

Christian sat heavily on the ground, "Okay; you got me, David. So now we're even."

David felt the beginning of a golf-ball size lump on his forehead. "You killed my head!"

"Sorry about that," Christian said with remorse. "I didn't know what grabbed me, and after Anna's talk of alligators, well…"

"Yeah, right. Well… I'll live," David said, not sounding convinced.

Watching the entire scene from higher ground, Anna attempted to stifle her laughter. "I'm sorry," she chuckled while waiting for Christian and David to climb the embankment. "You guys need to expend your energy in a different way. How about by packing?" Noticing David's head, her tone became more serious. "David, I have a first-aid kit in my backpack. Need me to look at your head?"

After gingerly touching the lump, he nodded. "I feel badly for any 'gator that tries to attack you, Christian!"

Once a cold compress had been applied to David's head, Anna, who had taken several first aid classes, assured him it wasn't serious. Although David complained about his discomfort, it had very little effect in diminishing his appetite. Anna watched as the two boys polished off what was left of the pancake and sausage breakfast Dr. Murphy made earlier.

Soon the three teens were busily at work splitting the chores. Anna took care of the cooking supplies and packed lunch. David and Christian cleared up the camping area, and David hung his sleeping bag out to dry. Thirty minutes later they were on their way down the river, having assured their father they had their two-way radios.

Christian positioned himself in the back of the canoe, with

David in the middle and Anna in the front. Although Anna did paddle, she paused frequently to take pictures. David's head continued to throb, so he was content to sit quietly while Christian's steady strokes propelled them forward.

"Anna will you please put your camera down and pick up an oar?"

Tossing her short brown hair, Anna swiveled around and snapped a photo of the boys without warning. "Smile!" she said after the picture had been taken.

"Anna! Cut it out," David said angrily.

"Come-on, Anna, row," Christian admonished, as the canoe headed crookedly toward the bank.

"No problem, I'm paddling," Anna reassured him, picking up the wooden oar. She quickly straightened their path and began to cut the water with strong, smooth strokes.

Christian adjusted his Marlin's cap to keep the sun out of his eyes, smiling to himself as he paddled. *I wonder how long Anna can go until she puts the oar down to take another shot*, he thought. *Can't blame her, though; it sure is pretty here.*

Almost an hour and several stops later, Christian pointed toward a boat ramp. "Here's where the fossil float we took a few years ago ended. This is as far down the river as we've ever been."

"David, have you been farther?" Anna asked.

"No, not too much because the river forks up ahead. The locals call the left fork 'the passage of no return.' Pretty neat name, huh?"

"What about the right fork?"

"It's called, the 'right fork'!"

"From one extreme to another," Christian retorted.

"Why do they call the left fork 'the passage of no return'?" Anna asked.

"Some say it's because of the giant man-eating alligators. But most say the river gets so shallow, bigger boats get stuck and can't return. You can pick the story you'd like to believe."

"There it is! Up ahead is the river fork," David enthusiastically pointed out.

"Let's take the left fork," both Christian and Anna called out simultaneously.

Laughing, Anna added, "Great minds think alike."

Without any protest from David, they proceeded down the river and hugged the left bank. Gliding uneventfully through patches of vegetation, they noted the muddy shoreline on either side. The gentle current made paddling enjoyable. No one spoke as they peacefully traveled on the deserted river, each caught up in their own thoughts.

Another twenty minutes revealed that the locals weren't entirely joking. Not more than thirty feet in front of the canoe the water level became extremely low.

"We need to be careful, Christian," David advised, noting the shallow water. "Hey! Look at that!" he pointed.

Christian let out a low whistle. "Wow, this is awesome! I've never seen so many 'gators!"

There, sunning themselves on the water's edge were about twenty alligators. Many lay motionless in the water, hidden from view with the exception of their eyes.

"Take a look at that!" David exclaimed as a six-foot long alligator slithered effortlessly into the river.

By now Anna had her camera out and ready. "Please get me a little closer, Christian," she pleaded, leaning precariously over the side of the boat to get an enhanced shot of an alligator slowly swimming toward them.

"This is close enough," returned Christian, equally fascinated by the reptiles. He planned to keep at a respectable distance.

"Let's drift with the current," David suggested, admiring the large gator close-up.

Utilizing her wide-angle zoom, Anna intently focused on another subject—an eight-foot alligator taking advantage of the cool shade on the shoreline.

Twenty-five feet turned into twenty, and then fifteen. Christian began to slowly paddle backward. "Hey, David, pick up Anna's oar and give me a hand. The water here is much deeper."

"This is great! I've got some really good pictures," Anna said, kneeling in the front of the canoe.

Half a dozen more shots and Anna was satisfied. She shifted and knelt on her seat to return the camera to its case in her backpack. Just then, the canoe suddenly struck something from beneath the murky water.

Much to Christian's horror it wasn't a log. "Hold on!" he shouted as he tried to steady the canoe.

The collision threw Anna off balance and she desperately grabbed at the sides of the canoe as it tipped. It was too late. The momentum carried her over the side. Splash! The warm water engulfed her as she sank into the thick silt. Pushing upward, she broke the water's surface, gasping for air. Paralyzed by fear she prayed in terror, *Dear Lord, Help me!*

Chapter 13
Missing!

Miraculously, the canoe remained upright. Anna continued thrashing as she attempted to tread water, and her soaked clothing and running shoes pulled her down like lead weights. Anna's mind went numb with the terrible realization that she was in the water with more than a dozen deadly alligators!

"I can't reach her; move up front!" Christian shouted to David. "I've got the canoe under control. You get up there and pull Anna in!" he ordered. Just in the brief moment he had stopped paddling, Christian noticed the current sweeping them further downstream. *If we're going to save Anna, I've got to control this canoe!* he determined, whipping the vessel around and frantically paddling toward his sister.

Meanwhile, Anna turned around to see how she could help herself. Having spotted an six-foot alligator heading her way, she stifled a scream. It wouldn't take long for the powerful thrust of the alligator's tail to propel it to her side. If she didn't act now, she would soon become its lunch. *Lord, help me!* Anna cried out, as a Scripture verse popped into her mind and quieted her fears. *The joy of the Lord is my strength.* Anna almost laughed. *Are you kidding, Lord? I know we're to be joyful in all things, but I don't think now is the time.* She knew she was loosing her mind. How could she feel joy when she was about to be devoured by a savage beast?

"Anna! Swim!" David yelled.

With adrenalin pumping, Anna's fear turned into energy. Realizing the canoe was coming toward her, she stroked frantically. Anna could sense the alligator effortlessly cutting through the water directly behind her. *Okay, Lord, I'll be joyful,* she surrendered, aware that God was in charge of her life even if this would be her end. The alligator opened its mouth and would be upon her in mere seconds.

Anna gauged the distance. *Too far! I'll never make it with ten more feet to go. It's hopeless!*

The alligator got within range and his huge jaws clamped down on Anna's—paddle! Christian thrust the oar into the alligator's gaping mouth, while David, on his knees, made a desperate lunge for Anna. Lifting her by the shirt, he unceremoniously hoisted her behind him into the middle of the canoe.

Before she could blink a second time, Anna found herself sprawled on the canoe floor. *I'm safe! But how can it be?* Anna's thoughts went in a hundred different directions. "Praise God!" she exclaimed through chattering teeth and shivering despite the hot day.

David sat down in the front with a thud, grabbed the oar and exhaled, "Yeah? Well it's not over!" Unhappy at the loss of its lunch, the alligator rammed the side of the canoe, rocking it precariously as water splashed from side to side.

"Whoa!" Christian shouted. He and David paddled with all their might to maneuver the boat away from the death trap. Never looking back, the two set their sights on the fork in the river and paddled furiously toward that goal. Anna huddled in the middle of the canoe, holding onto the seat with a white-knuckled grip. The alligator finally gave up the pursuit, and the boys slowed their pace only after they reached their destination safely.

"That was close!" Anna exhaled with trembling voice. "Thank you God for sparing me! There is truly joy in all things!"

"Joy? Are you okay, Anna?" David asked incredulously. "I don't call that a joyous event!"

Anna didn't answer, not yet ready to reveal what had transpired during the time she was in the water with the alligators.

For several minutes the boys paddled in silence. David, shaken by the near disaster, was the first to speak. "Man! You could have been killed!"

"Yes, but she's right. We need to thank God she wasn't," Christian added.

"I'm really glad you're okay, Anna," David added quietly.

His words were spoken with such heartfelt relief that Anna was taken aback even in the midst of her muddled thoughts. "I'm glad, too," she answered while shifting in the bench seat.

"I know what you all must be thinking," David ventured, "since we've never really gotten along in the past. To tell you the truth, I avoided the effort of trying to be friends since we rarely see each other. Besides, with all my dad has told me about you—well it's hard measuring up to such perfect cousins."

"You know how parents sometimes exaggerate," Anna consoled, adding, "You don't have to explain, David."

"No, I want to." David took a deep breath and continued to paddle. "It's just that you guys have a deep belief in God. I mean, what Anna said about being joyful is a completely foreign thought to me. You believe in Someone you can always count on to be there, and well, I don't."

"You can have faith, too," Christian piped up. "It's not an exclusive club, but free to whoever asks."

"Well, that's the problem... I don't believe like you do and sometimes I feel uncomfortable being around you," he admitted.

"Let's take it one step at a time," Anna said. Her tone warned Christian not to push too hard. *David had revealed more in the last few minutes than he ever has,* Anna thought. She felt led to share her experience with him. "You know, faith can come all at once or in little steps."

"What's the first step?" David asked, turning sincere blue eyes toward his cousin.

"The first step is to ask God for forgiveness of past sins and ask him to give you faith to believe."

David turned back around so he was facing forward and continued the rhythmic paddling. "I'll think about it," he finally replied.

"Having faith is a daily walk," Anna sighed, pausing. *This is going to be harder than I thought.* "You see, when I was in the water I was in shock; it appeared to be a hopeless situation. I felt the words come to me, actually from a song, 'the joy of the Lord is my strength' although I felt anything but joyous at that moment."

Anna's words hit David hard. He had so many questions he wanted to ask, but he narrowed it to one. "How could you have felt joyful in that situation? That's crazy!" David's stress on the last word was not lost on the Murphys.

Ignoring the barb, Anna continued. "Believe me, I argued with those thoughts in my mind, too. I couldn't believe they were leadings from the Lord—how could I be joyful about becoming 'gator bait!"

"And?" Christian encouraged his sister, knowing she was sharing a personal, emotional time with them because she hoped it might help David.

"I decided, at the last minute, that if God wanted me to be joyful, I would—no matter what the situation…and then you saved me, David!" Anna triumphantly claimed.

"Wow! What an awesome praise report, Anna!" Christian gave a hoot of delight, which alarmed two wading egrets, causing them to take flight across the river and into the sky.

"I'm disappointed that we didn't find anything significant down here," David said, effectively changing the subject. He'd have to think about what Anna said. The relationship she had with God was strange to him.

Christian agreed, "Yeah, but we can canoe down here again."

Anna, almost dry by this time, knew their trip was cut short because of her accident. "I'm so sorry I fell in, guys."

"It was an accident," David replied with a shrug. "Besides, it's time to head back. I want to visit my dad."

"I suppose we'll have to let our dad know what happened," Christian added, not relishing the fact. "But David is right, we need to get back to camp anyway. Let's pull over and eat our sandwiches in the canoe." While no one was very hungry, the simple task of eating was comforting after the adrenalin rush a few moments ago. Once finished, and with Anna safely and securely in the middle, the boys swiftly paddled back to camp.

Several hours and a safety lecture later, David finished a fast food dinner with the Murphys and went to the hospital. As he entered his father's room and peeked around the privacy curtains, David sighed in relief—glad to see his dad sleeping peacefully. *I do wish Dad were awake, though!* he thought as he pulled up a chair. *I really want a chance to talk to him alone!*

Gazing at his dad's sleeping form, David absently fingered the blanket covering his father. His thoughts wandered. Memories of his mother flashed through his mind—her sweet smile, her soft voice, her love, but most of all her belief in God that was as strong as his cousins'. He shook his head; it all seemed too easy! It was too child-like for him to believe in God. *Even though Dad says he believes in God, he never counts on anyone but himself. I've never heard him praying and he doesn't attend a church,* David thought as he remembered being taught to value facts and put his faith into what he could observe for himself.

Now, as he sat in confusion, David knew he couldn't stand the loss of his father, too. These hospital visits were unpredictable, and they conjured up painful memories of two years ago when it had been hard to cope with his mother's death.

Mike Murphy stirred, and his eyes fluttered open. He weakly smiled at David. "Hi," he rasped before launching into a series of coughs.

Startled at the sound of coughing, David shook his head and tried to clear his muddled thoughts. Wiping gathering tears from his eyes with the back of his hands, he mumbled, "Are...are you okay?"

His father rubbed his throat, recovering from the prolonged and violent coughing spell. David reached for the thermo mug with its bendable straw on the tray nearby and tenderly brought it to his father's lips. After a few swallows his dad pushed it away.

"I'm feeling so much better," Mike rasped, still sounding weak. "I thought I was at death's door for a while."

"Don't talk," David cautioned his dad.

Mike gave him another smile, "Who's the doctor?"

David could see signs of his Dad's sense of humor returning, always ready to joke. "Why I am, of course, and I think you need to rest," he said in his best imitation of a doctor's authoritive voice.

Mike nodded his head and relaxed against the pillow. In a mocking voice he replied, "Whatever you say, but your hair is a bit on the long side for a doctor."

Smiling, David raked his hands through his hair and pushed it off his forehead. "Do you want some dinner?"

"I already ate," Mike replied, and then asked, "Where's your Uncle Jack?"

"He's picking up a few supplies. He said to tell you he'd be in to see you a little later, along with Anna and Christian."

"I need to talk to Jack as soon as possible. There's some important information he needs to know related to the bones. Can you call him?"

David did as directed, immediately dialing his Uncle's cell number. After a brief conversation, he hung up. "He said he'd be here in thirty minutes, Dad."

A nurse came into the room with an air of authority, telling David he had to leave. "It'll only take a few minutes, Hon," she said in a rich southern accent. "I need to get him ready to see the doctor, okay?"

David had no choice but to agree. Walking down the hall to the waiting room, he looked over his shoulder. The doctor entered the room accompanied by two large male nurses. Hoping they wouldn't be long, David slumped into one of the well-worn cushioned chairs in the waiting room. He was anxious to spend more time with his father.

Fifteen minutes later and more than a dozen magazines, David muttered, "Why do doctors have to take so long?" Shuffling through another stack of periodicals, he found one of interest.

"What was that, Sonny?" A deep raspy voice came from across the room.

David jumped, wondering how long the old man had been sitting there. He warily replied, "Oh, nothing; it's just that Doctor DeWhite is taking forever."

"That he does. But you haven't been sitting here that long.

What's your name?" the old man asked as he set his magazine down.

"David Murphy."

Leaning both hands on his cane he answered, "Frank Wagner. Very nice to meet you. Is that your dad in Room 209?" he asked, carefully standing as if gauging his balance. He made his way over to David with slow and stiff steps and gingerly sat down in the seat beside him.

"Yes. How did you know?"

"My wife, Linda, is right across from his room in 208. Doctor DeWhite is her doctor too. He's slow but thorough. Can't say the same for those nurses, though. They come and go so fast. Makes me real nervous. I never let them be with my wife alone."

"Hmm, so you think there's something unusual going on?" David asked, deciding to humor the man. The conversation was better than sitting alone bored.

"That's exactly what I'm saying, young man, although not just one strange thing going on but several. Conspiracies, you know," he said, poking David with a bony finger. "You can't trust any of them big corporations. Especially the banks. But I wouldn't hold it past the insurance companies, either."

"Don't tell me. Let me guess. You carry all your money around in a briefcase," David kidded.

" 'Course I do," the thin old man replied, rather surprised and a little irritated that David had guessed his well-guarded secret.

David chuckled. *This man is like someone out of a movie!*

After another ten minutes of Mr. Wagner's ranting on the conditions of the world, David had enough. It was making him nervous. Deciding to see if the doctor had completed his task, David politely excused himself and headed down the hall. Upon arriving, he found the door to his father's room ajar. He pushed it open and tentatively entered. *I wonder if I should be in here*, David thought, pulling the curtain back. He stared down at an empty bed. His dad was gone.

Puzzled, David quickly headed to the nurses' desk. "Where did they take my dad?" he demanded, leaning over the counter to stare at the unsuspecting nurse. She gave him a blank look and announced, "Just a minute; I'm on the phone."

Not wanting to wait around, David tore down the hall, frantically looking for someone who could help. Mr. Wagner slowly walked toward him, leaning heavily upon his cane.

"Mr. Wagner!" David desperately called. "Have you seen my dad?"

"Why yes, those male nurses wheeled him down the hall. But don't worry young man. I asked where they were taking him."

"And?" David asked.

"They said to have some tests done."

"Oh," David said, suddenly feeling terribly childish for jumping to conclusions. All the talk of conspiracies had made him uneasy.

"There he is, Dr. DeWhite," the nurse called, pointing to David.

The doctor strolled toward him, hand extended. "Hello, David! I was looking for you."

"I've been in the waiting room for the past hour," David exaggerated.

"That's strange," the doctor said, frowning. "I was informed you had gone to dinner. No matter. I wanted to inform you of your father's amazing progress. He won't need the additional testing after all," Dr. DeWhite announced. "If your dad continues to improve, he can leave tomorrow. His recovery is nothing short of miracu—"

"What!" David exclaimed, cutting him off. "Dad's not in his room, and Mr. Wagner here just said the nurses took him to have tests run."

"I told you about nurses," Mr. Wagner cut in, shaking his head and waving his cane with vengeance.

"Calm down, son, they're probably new and misunderstood my instructions," Dr. DeWhite responded, disturbed. "We'll get to the bottom of this. Don't worry; everything will be fine. Nurse, please alert the lab that Mr. Murphy is not in need of tests," he ordered while handing her the chart in his hand.

"Yes, Doctor," the nurse nodded.

Turning to David, Dr. DeWhite smiled encouragingly. "How about waiting in your dad's room so I'll know where to find you," he suggested before he walked away.

"Where's the lab? Can I go there? David asked.

"No, it's off limits. But don't worry," the doctor called confidently over his shoulder, "we'll get this all straightened out!"

"Okay. I'll wait in his room," David sighed, upset at the turn of events. Mr. Wagner's words about the nurses still echoed in his mind.

Meanwhile, Dr. Murphy, Christian, and Anna arrived at the hospital. Although their shopping trip had been cut short by David's call, they did manage to pick up Anna's pictures and all necessary supplies. Taking the elevator to the second floor, the Murphys walked the short distance to Room 209 and knocked.

"Come in," David announced.

"Hey David. Where's Uncle Mike?" Anna asked, instinctively lowering her voice when she entered the room.

"I'm waiting here while Dr. DeWhite tries to figure out the answer to that very question," he answered irritably.

"What do you mean by 'figure out' where your dad is?" Dr. Murphy asked for clarification.

"A nurse came in, asked me to leave, and the next thing I knew some other nurses took him away for some tests he didn't need!" David said in a rush.

"Calm down and take a deep breath," Dr. Murphy consoled.

David slouched in his chair, deflated. Anna sat in the chair beside him while Christian perched on the empty bed.

Dr. Murphy walked to the window and looked out. "Who said he didn't need more tests?" he inquired

David quickly recounted most of the story. "How dumb is that?" he asked. "Then I saw Mr. Wagner in the hallway who said two male nurses took Dad for tests."

"Wait. Who is Mr. Wagner?" Christian asked.

"A man I met in the waiting room," David replied. "I think Dr. DeWhite is withholding information. He seemed upset."

"Oh well, you know how hospitals are," Christian said lightly, standing beside his dad at the window. *Something wasn't right,* he thought to himself. "I'm sure your father is fine," he said to encourage David.

David wasn't convinced but seemed more in control. "Yeah,

but what's taking so long?"

"I don't know," Christian said, clasping David's shoulder and giving him a big grin. "But they better hurry, or they'll have us to contend with!"

Anna smiled in spite of the situation. She knew her brother wasn't as confident as he appeared, but he was making David feel better and that's what counted for now.

"I can't wait around like this!" David announced. "I've got this feeling that something's wrong."

"Take it easy, son; we'll find him. You three stay here. I'll try to find out what's going on."

"Sure, Dad," Anna and Christian replied in unison.

David looked sullen and kept silent, his hands stuffed into the pockets of his jean shorts. *I can't loose my dad too... not like this!*

Dr. Murphy strode down the hall and in less than five minutes he was back. Before he could say anything, David bombarded him with questions. "Where is he? Is Dad okay? Can I see him?"

"Hold it now," Dr. Murphy sighed. "David, sit down."

David looked defiant for a second and then slumped into a chair. He raked his blond hair in frustration.

"It's quite puzzling," Dr. Murphy began. "No one seems to know your father's whereabouts—yet he has to be here somewhere!"

"So? Where is he then?" David demanded.

"He was last seen being wheeled down the hall by two male nurses. The doctor checked the lab, and Mike wasn't there. No one has seen the nurses either. The sheriff has been notified and they've already sent a patrol car here," Dr. Murphy finished.

David looked at his uncle in stunned silence. His blue eyes watered with unshed tears.

Dr. Murphy placed a hand on David's shoulder. "I believe the only thing we have left to do is pray." Bowing his head, he closed his eyes and led the three in a prayer for Mike's safety.

Two hours later Dr. Murphy and the three weary teens slowly made their way out of the hospital. The sheriff made a thorough search of the building and its surroundings. Having no further leads, the law enforcer sent the worried family back to camp with a promise to call. Apparently, Michael Murphy had been kidnapped!

Chapter 14
The Encounter

Thirty minutes later they were seated around the small table in the camper, talking over the hum of the air conditioner. "If someone had told me a hospital could be so careless with their patients, I would never have believed it," David remarked, cradling the mug of coffee before him.

Dr. Murphy felt the problem was more than carelessness and knew prayer was in order. "I think something sinister has transpired. Unfortunately your dad is caught in the middle of it."

Christian agreed. "I bet his disappearance is somehow related to the dig. Uncle Mike wanted Dad to oversee the process. For some reason, someone doesn't want Dad to talk to Uncle Mike."

"That doesn't make sense," David wailed in frustration.

"You said yourself that Uncle Mike wanted to see Dad," Anna gently reminded him.

"You're right," David said in agreement, "But I've been at the dig as much as Dad. The only problem I've heard him talk about is how over-zealous Jim can be. What could Dad possibly have to say to you, that he couldn't tell me?"

"At this point discussion is futile, but prayer is imperative," Dr. Murphy interjected. "Let's pray." Bowing their heads, the teens listened as their father led them in prayer. "Dear Heavenly Father, thank You for all the blessings You have given us. We ask You for the grace to make it through this difficult situation, and we release Mike into Your care. We pray for his safety and health, and for the authorities to be able to get to the bottom of this quickly. Give us Your peace through all of this, Lord, and draw our hearts closer to You because of it. In Jesus' name we pray, Amen."

Sheriff Ron Simons stopped by the camper that evening to briefly give an update on the investigation. So far they considered the two male nurses to be suspects and were acting upon information gleaned at the hospital. Upon parting, he assured them he would notify them if any new developments arose.

The following day, with the sun already low in the sky, Anna finished gathering firewood and twigs in preparation for a special camp-out down river. Noticing David's inability to concentrate on even the simplest of tasks and a growing depression, Dr. Murphy had agreed that a change in scenery might help—although he was initially reluctant to allow them to go.

After a fifteen-minute trip down river, Christian, Anna, and David quickly staked out a place to set up camp in the middle of a small clearing with a ten-foot drop-off to the water. It was just a few miles from the dig and within two-way radio contact. Climbing the sandy slope with gear in tow proved to be quite a challenge, yet no one seemed to mind. After their encounter with the alligators, they chose a place they knew would be reasonably safe. *I'm thankful we're not near the Passage of No Return*, Anna thought, shuddering as she reflected on their narrow escape.

Having erected the tents with little effort and in record time, the teens soon tackled other tasks. With the making of an encircled fire pit, the last touch on the makeshift campsite was complete, and they all pitched in to cook dinner over the open fire. All enjoyed the simple meal of hot dogs, canned beans, and chips, although dinner was somber and quiet with everyone deep in thought.

David had insisted on calling his uncle from time to time for possible updates. No one complained. Again, David unclipped his

110

radio and pushed the call button and waited for Uncle Jack to respond. "That's strange; my signal light is off," David complained. "That usually means the batteries are dead," answered Christian.

"I'll check mine," Anna offered, unclipping her radio. To her dismay, she realized hers were dead.

"That was smart of us!" Christian exclaimed, as he noted his radio had lost power. "There was no need for all of us to keep our radios on at the same time, especially when we're all together."

"The battery usually lasts eight hours," David insisted, clicking it on and off in disbelief.

"Yes, but they've been used repeatedly for days," Anna reminded him.

"I can't believe we didn't replace the batteries earlier when we had the chance," Christian said grimly as he stared into the fire.

David panicked. "Did you bring extra batteries?" he queried, worried he'd miss important news pertaining to his father.

Both Anna and Christian shook their heads.

"I've got to get back to the dig site, now!" David insisted. *What if something awful has happened?* David couldn't voice his thoughts out loud.

"I'll go with you," Christian offered. "We'll get more batteries and come back. The trip here took about fifteen minutes. Going back will be faster without gear to weigh us down."

Anna opted to stay. *I'd rather stay here alone than brave the river at night!* she thought.

After securing the supplies so raccoons couldn't get to them, Anna relaxed. Night crept slowly upon her and she had a chance to take some stunning pictures of the setting sun. After dark, she decided to stargaze. *Wow*, Anna thought, *the sky is so clear and the stars are so brilliant tonight.* Lying on a blanket, she was able to easily pick out the North Star and the Big Dipper. She eventually located Orion, known as Bootes the Herdsman, Virgo the Virgin and Spica one of the major stars in that constellation. Anna was glad her mother purchased the Creation Astronomy unit study for their science class that year. One of the authors, Jill Whitlock, had given a

111

wonderful presentation on the topic. Having learned the original Greek and Hebrew meanings behind the stellar names, Anna was able to recognize the awesome story of the Gospel message in the stars.

Sitting up, Anna instinctively knew why she had purposely kept her mind busy—to stop all the thoughts that kept surfacing. There were still so many unanswered questions, and they were nowhere close to being resolved. Where does Lauren fit into the mystery? And Uncle Mike. Why would anyone want to kidnap him? It doesn't make sense. Not to mention Arcadia Man! Is he authentic or just another fraud? Anna pondered. She wished she had more experience with solving mysteries.

Restlessly, Anna stood to stretch. She stirred up the fire and placed another log on the dying embers. Crickets chirped and an occasional owl hooted as Anna entered her tent. Rummaging through her backpack, she found her flashlight and checked her watch. The boys should have been back half an hour ago! As Anna slipped out of the tent, the hairs on the back of her neck suddenly rose. Glancing around, she called, "Christian? David?"

No one answered but she heard the rustle of leaves. Anna flashed her light in the direction where she knew Christian and David would come. The powerful beam cut across the darkness, but she saw nothing unusual. The welcome sound of chirping crickets had abruptly ceased and the silence made her uneasy.

"Come on, Christian, this isn't funny. I know you're there," Anna stated angrily.

The eerie silence broke when a dog barked in the distance. Anna shivered as she scanned the moonlit river. Shadows. There were too many shadows.

A twig snapped. *What was that?* Anna thought as she whirled around and barely stifled a scream. Not more than ten feet in front of her towered a seven-foot tall, fur-covered giant of a man! A pair of green eyes seemed to glow from under his thick hair. His face was hidden in the shadows of his hood.

Wildly waving his arms, a deep voice roared, "Get away! I don't want you here! Go back to where you belong."

"Who…who are you?" Anna asked in a small, shaky voice.

"Leave well enough alone," he hissed.

Anna's fear turned into anger, and she took a step closer. "You have no right to threaten me!"

"Tell your people to leave!" the giant hissed.

Losing her nerve, Anna retreated. "What are you talking about?"

Raising a hatchet high above his head, the giant didn't answer, only his menacing gaze remained fastened on her.

Anna screamed as she turned to run. Taking several steps, she collided with someone and swung out at the dark figure as it tried to grab her.

"Let go of me!" Anna fought to no avail.

"Hey! Watch it, Anna, it's me."

Anna let out a gasp. "Christian! L-Look!" She grasped his shirt to spin him around to see the giant, but it had vanished. Although only seconds had passed, the huge figure was nowhere to be seen.

"Where's David?" Anna cried, looking around. "David! Is this a cruel joke?" Anger wiped away any fear she'd felt.

"What are you talking about?" David asked as he approached over the embankment.

Anna studied his face. Seeing his puzzlement, she quickly related what had transpired.

"It wasn't me. I just got here," David defended as he stepped past Christian to stand in front of both Murphys. "Christian, tell her!"

"He's right, Anna. This wasn't anything we cooked up."

"Then why did Christian come up the embankment over here from the right instead of the left?" Anna demanded with hands on her hips.

Christian raised his hands in defeat. "Ok, you caught us, we were going to sneak around and come up on you from behind. When we heard you calling, we figured you saw us and were going to come out. That's when we heard you yell."

"So if it wasn't you guys...then who was it? Someone playing a joke?" Anna's uneasiness returned.

"Doesn't sound very funny to me. What did he mean by 'leave well enough alone'?"

"I have no idea," Anna replied, "but I sure wish I knew."

"Are you all right now, Anna?" Christian asked.

"Yeah, I'm okay."

Minutes later, the three huddled around the campfire talking about possible suspects. While making s'mores, they discussed possible meanings behind the mysterious man's cryptic statement and could not seem to shake the feeling that they were being watched.

"There's got to be a rational explanation," Christian stated as he skewered another marshmallow onto his stick and placed the tip into the glowing embers. "Are you sure he was covered with fur?"

"Well, I didn't see his whole body; he just appeared out of nowhere!" Anna exclaimed as she situated her toasted marshmallow between two graham crackers and a chocolate square.

"Was he referring to our camping here? Or did he mean the excavation? Which does he want stopped?" Christian questioned, not expecting an answer. "Why would he care if we continued to dig or not?"

"The only way any of this would make sense," David responded, "is if he knew what we were excavating. But that's impossible because we've kept tight security."

"Maybe he feels that we're trespassing," Christian replied.

"That guy was really bizarre. Maybe he's just naturally strange and his threat was meaningless," Anna offered.

"I'll say!" David agreed. "In all my traveling, that definitely was the weirdest thing I've ever heard." He took another large bite of his sticky dessert. "Nothing like this has ever happened to me before, until now," David confessed.

Anna and Christian exchanged knowing looks over the campfire. They, too, had been mixed up in some strange things lately. When neither of them responded, David glanced from Christian to Anna. Mumbling around his mouthful, he asked, "What did I miss?"

"Well," Anna began in a storyteller's voice, "It all started when we were in the Florida Keys on vacation." Some of her uneasiness subsided as she told David the story of their adventures on Key Largo, pausing from time to time as Christian interjected his version of the story. She recounted every detail, from the free trip on the charter fishing boat, to the FBI helicopter takeover, and finally to the explosion.

Once Anna had finished her narrative, David gave a low whistle. "I can't believe it! You're kidding, right?"

"It was some trip," Christian agreed, shaking his head in wonder.

"You've got to be exaggerating," David stated, looking at them in disbelief.

"Hey! I know! We have proof," Anna brightly responded. "We can look at the pictures I took when we get back. I just had two rolls of film developed."

"Why doesn't that surprise me?" David laughed. "But why didn't you tell me any of this earlier?"

"I guess we never had a chance with all that has been going on here. Besides, I've barely glanced at the pictures," Anna explained.

"That's not the oddest part, though. Remember us telling you about Lauren, the captain's first-mate?"

"Yes, what about her?" David asked.

"She seemed so nice aboard the boat, it's hard to believe she might possibly be mixed up in criminal activity," Christian explained. "Anna and I saw her here in Arcadia—not just once but twice!"

"That's no coincidence!" David exclaimed.

"We saw her get into a SUV . . ."

"With this really good-looking guy driving," Anna interjected.

Rolling his eyes, Christian continued. "As I was saying, after Lauren got into the SUV, we decided to follow her. She ended up at a motel on Fifth Street."

"You actually followed her!" David said astonished. His cousins were becoming more of a surprise to him by the minute.

"Yeah, Christian and I did the whole spy thing, including hiding behind the building next door," Anna said, giggling. "It's our first real mystery!"

David mused, "I wonder if Lauren's here because of you guys?"

Anna frowned, "Why would she be following us? We haven't done anything wrong, unless you consider accepting a free fishing trip as illegal. She seemed friendly, almost like the girl-next-door type. I'm still hoping she's not mixed up in anything sinister."

"Well, if you don't believe what happened to us, you're never going to believe some of the unusual things that have happened in the past on this very river," Christian announced mysteriously. He flashed Anna a smile.

"No! Not that!" Anna laughed. "David, you won't believe this—Christian researched Arcadia and found information about an old mystery dealing with a guy and a reward. What was his name? Something Stanley?"

"Reward for who?" David asked with interest. "What did he do?"

"His name is Nelson Stanley," Christian explained. He told David about the smugglers and how they kept stolen goods in a shed close by the river—purposefully omitting the fact that the event occurred thirty years ago.

"Cool! I can't wait 'till that reward is posted. I'd like to catch the guy, no matter where he is," David stated excitedly. "And just when I thought Arcadia was a boring town!"

"Anna thought the same thing, that is, until I told her it happened over three decades ago," Christian amended, waiting for David's reaction.

David flung a sticky marshmallow at Christian, accurately hitting his mark squarely on the cheek.

"Good one, David," Anna laughed as Christian peeled the sticky morsel off his cheek and smiled. "He purposely left that part out when he told me the story earlier! Apparently it's still an unsolved mystery. I do wonder what ever happened to Nelson, though."

"You never know, Nelson could be out there right now, lurking in the bushes, waiting for the right time to smuggle more artifacts into this unsuspecting town," Christian said, his voice lowered to imitate a spooky tone.

"I think you've read too many mystery books, Christian," Anna admonished.

David was about to add to Christian's story when they heard a large branch crack. "What was that?"

"I don't know, and I'm not going anywhere to find out," Anna whispered. Looking over her shoulder to the left, she saw the palmetto bushes stir, and shuddered. Anna thought about the man who tried to scare her earlier before mysteriously disappearing. She scooted closer to Christian.

"It's probably just an animal in the woods or the wind ruffling the palmetto bushes," Christian said in response to David's questioning look.

David glanced around apprehensively. "There's not much wind tonight."

"Then it was probably just an animal," Christian countered with more conviction than he felt. "See? It's gone."

Anna wasn't convinced, but she had no better explanation.

She refused to let her imagination entertain the thought that the strange man might have returned.

Chapter 15
Trouble

After a restless and sleepless night Anna felt groggy. While tossing in her tent, her overactive imagination had continuously played out various scenarios of the mystery. Who was the mysterious handsome driver of the SUV? Was it Lauren's husband? What was his part in the mystery? Who had screamed in the motel? It didn't sound like a lady, but could it have been Lauren in trouble? Why had the boat blown up in the Keys? What was so secretive about the dig, and most important of all, where was Uncle Mike, and was he safe? Anna's thoughts had run rampant, and even shifted to David.

At least David's less disagreeable lately. It must be hard having his father missing—and trying to cope with all this without faith! Thanking the Lord for the gift of faith, Anna decided it was time to get up.

While negotiating the small space in her one-man tent, Anna changed from her rumpled T-shirt into a cool, sleeveless tank. Crawling on all fours, she pulled open the tent flap and alighted. Glad to be out of the tent's confines, Anna stretched and worked out some of the kinks in her back. Opening her portable umbrella style chair, she sat in front of the burned out campfire, glad for the opportunity to pray. Anna enjoyed spending moments such as these in quiet contemplation and offering her day to the Lord. She waited for the appointed time to radio her dad. Finally, at 7 A.M., Anna pushed the call button on her two-way radio and began to pace as she waited for a response.

Christian came out of the tent yawning. Taking one look at his sister, he stated, "You look like I feel."

"Thanks, its great having a brother who tells the truth," Anna sarcastically rejoined. "I couldn't sleep; I kept wondering if that guy was going to come back."

Before Christian could respond, they heard the return ring of their father's radio.

Anna flounced into her chair. "Morning, Dad," she said, trying to sound more cheerful than she felt.

"Hi Anna," her father replied and then sighed.

Anna glanced at Christian. By the tone of their father's voice, they both instantly knew something was amiss.

Prodding, Christian urged, "Ask him what's wrong—any news about Uncle Mike?" Christian feared the worst.

Speaking into the handset she asked, "What's going on, Dad? Have you heard anything about Uncle Mike?"

Sighing heavily into the radio, Dad answered, "I wish we had, but no, the sheriff's leads have turned into dead-ends. To make matters worse, there's been vandalism and theft here. How are you all? Is everything all right?"

"We're fine, Dad," Anna reassured. There was no need to add to his concern with the story of her unexpected visitor.

"I think you'd better pack up and return here immediately," Dad responded. "We'll need all the extra help we can get today."

An hour later, once they arrived at the dig site, the three teens saw what had been so upsetting. Debris was scattered all about the campsite. Plastic bags, some with labels, were strewn haphazardly on the ground, and chaos characterized the once orderly area.

"There's still no news about Dad?" David immediately asked before noticing his surroundings. Once he did, his mouth gaped open in astonishment. "What happened to the tents?" He made his way over to inspect the slashed canvas.

Dr. Murphy's gaze was serious. "Sorry, David. There is no news about your father, and as you can see, vandals visited in the night, slashed Harry's tent, and stole many of our tools."

"What?" They exclaimed in unison.

"What about Arcadia Man?" David questioned while running toward the partially covered form of the fossilized remains. His keen eyes noted the additional excavation work completed on its lower torso.

"He's the only thing that's 'fine' in this entire campsite," Jim stressed. He appeared frazzled as he determinedly strode through the clearing. "For whatever reason, they spared him!" Shaking his head, he continued. "I can't for the life of me understand who would do such a thing. In all my years on excavation sites, I have never seen such utter disregard for the preservation of our research into antiquity!"

Christian looked at Anna, rolling his eyes and muttering, "All his 'years'? You'd think he was fifty and not in his thirties."

Jim aimlessly walked around the site and finally sat dejectedly by Harry, who was perched on a fallen log and sipping a cup of coffee. Slumped over, Jim placed his head in his hands and moaned.

"Jim, are you okay?" Christian asked, bewildered. *Get a grip, man!* he thought.

Dr. Murphy answered for Jim. "I think we're all suffering from shock. Realizing someone was walking around the campsite while we were sleeping is unnerving, but slashing tents? Our lives could have been in danger!"

"To mention nothing of the delay this is going to cause! We'll be way behind our schedule," Jim whined.

"Did you hear anything in the night, Dad?" Christian asked, tired of Jim's complaining.

"Around 3 A.M. I heard someone walking outside my tent. I presumed it was either Harry or Jim, but I got up anyway to investigate. It's a good thing I did. When I walked around the tent, I saw a man—well you'll find this difficult to believe—he was dressed in fur!"

Anna gasped when she heard her dad's description of the man. *The man in the woods! It must be the same one who warned*

121

me to leave. Although wanting to tell him about her encounter, Anna waited for the right moment.

"At first I thought it was some type of hairy animal. I couldn't make out any features. Unfortunately, he made off with some of our tools before I scared him away," Dr. Murphy admitted. "He apparently knows these woods well to travel them at night. I tried to follow him but it was useless. The tents weren't slashed at that time, so he must have returned later to do it."

"That guy was really busy last night," Christian said, "and not just here."

"You saw him, too?" Dr. Murphy asked with alarm.

"Well, not exactly, but he gave Anna a scare," Christian replied as he informed his father of the details. "But he mysteriously disappeared before we arrived."

"What time was that?" his father asked.

"It was around eight when David and I got back to the camp," Christian responded.

David nodded in agreement. "We didn't see him, but Anna did."

Dr. Murphy gave Anna a questioning look, worry evident on his face.

"I'm okay—really, Dad!" Anna reassured.

"Thank God!" Dr. Murphy stated, walking over to his daughter and placing a protective arm around her shoulders. "Did he do or say anything?"

"Yes," Anna began. Encircled in her father's protective arms, she felt confident to speak about the events. "The man spoke forcefully about wanting us to leave. I assume he was speaking about the dig because he said 'tell your people to leave.' The boys and I discussed this but we can't figure out why he would be so angry. Whatever the reason, it was obvious he doesn't want anyone around."

"After the events of last night, what is obvious is his wish for us to stop digging—something you can't do without tools," Dr. Murphy replied grimly.

"Maybe he wanted to warn the kids," Jim said, "thinking he would scare them into coming back and telling us. When they didn't leave, he took matters into his own hands."

Harry forcefully added, "I, for one, think we should take his advice and leave. After all, who knows if the guy is a psycho and what he'll do next."

"Leave? Have you lost it, man?" Jim asked, incredulously. "Leaving is not an option!" he stated emphatically, appalled anyone would even suggest such a ridiculous notion.

"But why does he have an interest in this dig?" Dr. Murphy wondered.

"Maybe this guy somehow figured out that we're excavating Arcadia Man," David supplied. "But, how would he know the significance of this find?"

Dr. Murphy rubbed the back of his neck. "How, indeed."

"Impossible!" Jim exclaimed.

"Perhaps, but we have to look at all the possibilities," Dr. Murphy insisted. "The sheriff should be notified of our intruder."

"No!" Jim exclaimed. "No one is allowed to know what we've found, and that goes for the authorities. The damage was minimal and I'm sure this man is perhaps a nature buff, wanting to preserve…the…environment," he lamely finished.

That would be laughable if this weren't such a tragic moment! Christian thought, exchanging looks with Anna and David who shook his head incredulously.

"Alright. For now we'll keep this to ourselves. If there is a next time, I will call the sheriff and ask for 24-hour surveillance," Dr. Murphy warned. "This stranger may be dangerous, just as Harry suggested."

"I think we're making a big mistake in staying," Harry lamented.

Jim stood up and began to pick up some of the items strewn haphazardly around the site. "This is getting us nowhere! All we're doing is guessing. After cleaning up I'm going into town," he announced and hesitated before adding, "We need tools and supplies to finish this dig."

"We'll finish the clean-up here, Jim," Dr. Murphy offered. "If you'd like, take Harry with you. There's not much the rest of us can do except clean up and try to repair the tents. If you could buy patching material, that would be a great help."

"We can do that," Jim replied, still obviously agitated. He continued to pick up items as he walked toward his tent to prepare for the trip into town. "Harry, don't dawdle, man. Come on; let's go!" he called over his shoulder. Within minutes, the powerboat was headed back to the marina.

"What was Jim's problem?" Christian asked his father, shaking his head as he pondered Jim's strange behavior.

"I'm not sure, but I'm suspecting his reputation is tied up in this dig. You see if this specimen is a missing link, Jim Johnson will be a renowned name in the scientific community. He will be known as the man who helped excavate and identify the ape-like creature-to-man link. If the dig is sabotaged and Arcadia Man ruined, Jim's hope of making it into the history books is like-wise ruined."

"Jim has always been a meticulous scientist," David explained. "We've worked with him many times, and he can get defensive about his findings. As you can see, excavating is very tedious and time consuming. None of us want our research destroyed."

Dr. Murphy smiled at David. "You sound just like your father. I'm proud of your dedication to this project. Understand, though, that I'd expect all of Arcadia Man to be excavated and thoroughly lab tested before any age related conclusions are made."

"Agreed," David said, before adding, "but by all appearances and with the measurements we've obtained so far you have to admit he falls within the dimensions of the missing link."

"Well," Dr. Murphy mused, "by all known physical appearances it does, but sometimes looks may be deceiving. Now, let's get this place cleaned up."

It took the remainder of the morning and part of the afternoon to pick up the debris and repair sections of the tents as best they could. Another call from the sheriff yielded no additional information concerning Mike's disappearance. Sighing, Dr. Murphy pressed the end button. "Sorry, David," he replied, shaking his head in response to David's unanswered questions.

"Can't we hire our own private detective, Uncle Mike?" David asked. "If my dad's been kidnapped, why haven't we received a ransom note? And what could the criminals possibly want? It's not like we're rich," he huffed.

"I've already made some inquiries in that direction," Dr. Murphy said, rubbing the back of his neck in frustration. "You're correct David; if he's been kidnapped as it appears he has, why haven't we been notified? No, I think there is something more sinister going on, and your father may have just been in the wrong place at the wrong time."

"Like what? If someone is after Dad wouldn't they be after me, too?" David challenged.

"I hope not," his Uncle returned somberly. "Look, David, I don't have any answers—just hundreds of questions. The best thing we can do right now is pray and keep busy working. Spending time in futile worry isn't going to bring your father back."

"You don't really think David is in any danger," Anna commented, surprised her father didn't deny David's claim.

"The only thing I know, Anna, is that while we are on this dig, none of us is completely safe. Last night is proof of that," Dr. Murphy sighed. Someone doesn't want us digging here, and it appears they've removed the lead scientist involved. If we can find the fur-clad man, we might have a chance of finding my brother. In the meantime, we need to leave it to the authorities. No matter what Jim thinks, I am going to follow up on this vandalism."

"Have you told Mom about Uncle Mike, yet?" Christian asked.

Heading to his tent, Dr. Murphy held up his cell phone stating, "No, and I guess I've put this off long enough. I need to inform your mother of what has transpired, and I dread this call. I may be awhile."

"In the meantime we'll clean up," Christian volunteered.

Thirty minutes later David announced he was taking a break. "Anyone care to join me?" he asked as he up-righted a chair and fell heavily into it.

"I'm in!" Christian replied and sat across from his cousin in another chair. "Hey, Anna, let's see your pictures."

"Okay!" Anna agreed, always happy for a chance to share her photos. She hurried into her tent to retrieve them.

Christian and David grabbed a chair for Anna, and placed theirs on either side of hers. They were interested in the best vantage point from which to view the pictures.

As she walked to take her seat in the middle, Anna laughingly teased, "You two don't want to miss a single, wonderful picture of mine, do you!"

"Anything is preferable to cleaning," Christian laughingly rejoined.

Anna seated herself and removed the pictures from the envelope. Carefully holding the edges, she began flipping through the pile, mindful of both Christian and David as she began a monologue of the sequence of events.

"Wow look at that huge fish!" David admired. The picture included Christian proudly holding up his Red Snapper.

"It was big!" Christian agreed. "Do you like to fish, David?"

"I love it, but I don't get much of a chance. Dad and I spend most of our time with a trowel in hand," he admitted.

"Well," Christian invited, "maybe you can join us next time we take a fishing trip."

"I'd like that," David responded warmly.

Anna smiled. *What a difference! Things with David have certainly improved.*

"Come-on Anna, let's go to the next picture," Christian urged.

"Look at Andy; isn't he cute?" Anna flipped to the next one, admiring the shot of her little brother. Searching through a few pictures, she finally got to the ones where she and Christian were on deck.

"What are these supposed to be of?" David asked. The previous pictures, having been taken with photographic expertise, were dramatically different from the latter ones depicting only half of the sky and deck.

"Oh, I took those when Christian and I went up on deck," Anna answered. "The boat was moving so fast and the ride was so rough it made my hand unsteady."

Shuffling through several unidentifiable pictures in the pile, Anna finally found one she recognized. "Here's a photo of the boat

126

we followed. And let's see, what's this?"

"Who's that guy?" David asked, pointing to the picture.

Anna gasped, "Christian! It can't be—we've seen this guy!"

Christian squinted, taking the photo from Anna's outstretched hands. "I don't believe this! This is the guy that was driving the SUV Lauren got into the other day!" Sudden comprehension dawned and Christian's face paled. "But that can't be the same man. The boat and all the people on it were destroyed in the explosion!"

Chapter 16
The Leak

The three teens sat in stunned silence for a moment before they all began talking at once.

"This is impossible."

"Pictures don't lie!" Anna countered.

"But how did he get off the boat? We saw it explode!"

"How would I know? I just took the shot," Anna said, looking perplexed.

"Haven't you examined these pictures before?" David asked.

"No, because we've been too busy. Truthfully, I forgot all about them!" Anna admitted, noticing David's frown.

"If we had known earlier," Christian inserted, "we could have shown them to the authorities. As it stands now, we don't know the whereabouts of the mystery man—or Lauren for that matter. We saw them enter the motel, but that doesn't mean they're still there," Christian said in a rush.

"Will you guys calm down?" David interrupted, trying to follow the conversation. "What's the big deal, anyway?"

"Okay," Anna began with a deep breath, "let me try and explain why this is so incredible. If the man on the boat in this picture is the same man we saw in town, then there's more going on here than meets the eye!"

"Something very suspicious!" Christian added.

"Do you think there is any connection between that and the dig?" David questioned, intrigued by the possibility. "Why else would this man be in town? There isn't anything else going on of historical and scientific importance."

"I doubt that," Anna said, smiling to soften her words. "On the other hand, David may have a point. No one is supposed to know of this excavation."

"Maybe they want to steal Arcadia Man and sell him to the highest bidder!" David insisted. "They would be trading in stolen goods. Some fossils are quite valuable."

"Wait!" Christian held up his hand, "I think you may have something…"

"You don't really think this guy actually plans to steal a fossil!" Anna protested, surprised her brother's words echoed her own thoughts.

"No," Christian clarified, "That's not what I'm thinking. We don't know what the guys on the other boat did, but whatever it was, it was serious enough to bring the FBI into the chase."

"Do you think it could involve drugs?" David asked, once again intrigued.

"No, because the DEA would be involved," Christian replied.

"DEA?" Anna asked

"Drug Enforcement Agency," both boys answered in unison.

"Oh," Anna said. "So, if not drugs then what?"

"What does the FBI investigate?" Christian asked.

"I'm not sure," David attempted, "but don't they deal with violations of federal laws?"

"Yes," Christian said. "Like espionage, bank robbery, security issues, sabotage, international crime…maybe this is…an international crime ring. What do you think, Anna, 'sound familiar?"

"The Arcadia mystery from that newspaper article!" Anna gasped.

"Exactly!" Christian agreed.

The whooshing of a helicopter's approach interrupted their

conversation. Hovering directly overhead, it was just high enough to keep things from blowing, but low enough to be a nuisance.

Dr. Murphy came out of his tent. "What's going on here?"

Shielding their eyes from the sun, the Murphys looked up and tried to read the inscription on the helicopter. "It's the television news crew!" David exclaimed, recognizing the call letters.

"What would a television crew be doing here?" Anna questioned. *Oh no! They found out about the fossil!* she thought, answering her own question. *I just pray they don't jump to conclusions!* Deep down, however, she knew the possibility of that occurring was very likely. The media would assume an evolutionary origin and she could imagine how this might damage her father's career as a creation scientist.

Dr. Murphy's voice boomed above the roaring of the rotors. "Everyone! Quick! Give me a hand!" he shouted while running to the dig site. He instinctively knew the media was on a hunt for pictures of Arcadia Man. "Somehow information about our dig must have leaked out!" he shouted.

The teens quickly followed and helped secure the tarps which already covered the exposed portion of Arcadia Man. Upon finishing, they looked up to see they were no longer alone. The noise from the helicopter had been the perfect cover. Descending upon the site were several groups of men and women. Some came by boat from the river, while others came from the property line two miles behind an old deserted home.

If this inconvenience had occurred at any other time, the scene would have been humorous. Many of the reporters were clad in office wear. The women especially were having a difficult time walking with high heels in the sand.

"Hold it, hold it!" yelled an excited familiar voice. "What do you think you're doing?" Jim and Harry had returned. By the looks on their faces, they were not pleased to see the crowd that had convened in their absence. Harry immediately ducked into his tent, wanting no part of the ruckus. Apparently the helicopter had taken all the film needed and decided to move on.

"What is the meaning of this?" Jim demanded, looking at Dr.

131

Murphy accusingly.

"Perhaps you could tell us?" Dr. Murphy replied cynically. The standoff was interrupted by voices of reporters all clamoring to be heard. A few of the more vocal ones pushed forward to ask questions.

"Excuse me? Who's in charge here?" one reporter challenged.

"I'd like to speak with a…um…Dr. Jack Murphy," said another, looking through her notes.

"Is it true that Dr. Michael Murphy is missing?"

"What is it that you're researching here?"

"What have you unearthed?"

"Is the rumor correct?"

"Have you found the missing link?" demanded another.

Jim Johnson gained control of his emotions and smoothly took charge as if he had rehearsed this moment during sleepless nights. Holding up his hands as if orchestrating a band, he signaled for silence.

The crowd of otherwise unruly journalists hushed and listened while the Murphys watched in amazement—too horrified to interrupt.

"Ladies and gentlemen, all your questions will be answered in due time. First I'd like to introduce myself and my assistants."

"Boy, who died and made him king?" Christian huffed quietly.

"Shh!" Anna urged. "Let's see how he handles this."

David stepped forward, glaring at Jim before announcing, "Hello. My name is David Murphy; Dr. Michael Murphy is my father. He is the supervisor and in charge of this excavation. Unfortunately, he is recovering from an illness, and therefore, unable to answer your questions at this time. His assistant," David paused for emphasis, gesturing toward a startled Jim, "Mr. Johnson, is unfortunately unable to answer any of your questions, for if he did his job and reputation would be in jeopardy. Now will you all please leave, because if you don't, the sheriff's department will be alerted and you will be escorted off this private property."

"Way to go, David!" Christian quietly cheered, proud of his cousin.

The reporters seemed to ignore his comments and continued

asking questions in their insistence to uncover the story.

"David? Could you offer a statement verifying whether there is any truth to the rumor that your father has been kidnapped? Have you received a ransom note?"

David responded with silence, shaking his head defiantly and glaring at the reporter.

"How about the claim that you've unearthed the missing link that will finally prove evolutionary claims?" another asked.

"We just want to take a few pictures," a photojournalist requested.

David shook his head. "Please!" He held up his hand for silence.

Dr. Murphy walked up behind his nephew, putting a hand on his shoulder. "Ladies and gentlemen, the sheriff has been called." He held up his cell phone for emphasis. "And he is sending over his deputies to patrol the area. As scientists, we have special permission to be here on this private land. I'm sorry you'll have to leave willingly or you will be escorted off the premises. The decision is yours."

"What are you hiding?" one disgruntled reporter shouted.

"When we're ready to share our research and findings with the public, the media will be notified," Dr. Murphy returned. "Now, please! We expect the authorities any time."

As if on cue, several deputies arrived and escorted the reporters from the property. The group of discontented journalists slowly exited, except one.

Taking pictures from every possible angle, one photojournalist managed to sneak close enough to attempt lifting the tarp of Arcadia Man before David interrupted. "Excuse me sir, the excavation is off limits." The scowling man left.

Good thing Dad had the presence of mind to cover the fossil, Anna thought. Turning toward her father she asked, "I wonder who told them about the dig?"

"It was bound to come out sooner or later," Dr. Murphy replied, watching the group retreat and shaking his head sadly. "And I have my suspicions about why it was sooner."

Whatever those suspicions were, her father decided now was

not the time to voice them. "One thing is certain," Dr. Murphy added quietly, "the sooner we find my brother, excavate Arcadia Man, and leave—the better I'll feel!"

Chapter 17
This Old Man

"We'd best turn back," David warned, glancing apprehensively at the darkening sky.

Although Christian, Anna, and David had been canoeing upstream all morning, the thought of turning back this soon seemed disappointing.

"But I haven't taken enough pictures," Anna argued.

David laughed. "Why doesn't that surprise me? I've never seen anyone take so many. First there was the picturesque oaks with Spanish moss, then the sunning turtles, then the..."

"Okay, okay," Anna interrupted, giggling. "So, it doesn't take much to get me excited about photography."

"Excited about photography?" David teased. "Obsession would be a more accurate description."

Anna laughed good-naturedly. "Thanks, I'll take that as a compliment! I'm glad Dad allowed this break from routine."

"That's only because he didn't have the time to take pictures of the surrounding area himself," Christian offered.

David scanned the sky once again. "Well, I think a big storm is headed our way."

Christian nodded his head. "I agree with David; we'd better

turn back." As if on cue, they saw lightning flash in the distance followed by the low rumbling of thunder. "If we turn around now we can make it to the excavation site before it pours," Christian urged, expertly turning the canoe and heading downstream.

With disappointment, Anna returned her camera to its case and placed it in a waterproof plastic bag, then into her padded backpack for extra protection. She picked up her oar and helped paddle.

"At least we don't have to fight the current," Christian said, trying to cheer her up.

"Yes, and we do need the rain since it's been so dry," Anna agreed, trying to make the best of the situation.

"But also remember," David commented, "that rain can jeopardize the safety of the fossil. Hopefully, it won't pour too hard!" He nervously looked up at the sky, not used to the sudden torrential Florida storms.

Less than ten minutes later the darkened sky blocked the sunlight, making it seem hours later than mid-afternoon. The wind began to pick up as the canoe made its passage toward the camp.

"I hate to mention the obvious but I don't think we're going to make it all the way back," David announced as a large raindrop fell on his face. "How about finding a place to wait it out?" he suggested.

"Good idea. Keep your eyes open. I think I saw a cabin somewhere near here," Christian piped up.

One drop became two, which multiplied to four. Soon it was raining in sheets and drenching the teens.

"Hey!" Anna cried, "Look over there! See that light?" She stood to get a better look. "Maybe whoever lives there will let us ride out the storm."

"Anna, sit down, or you'll capsize us! Yes, we see it!" David acknowledged. "Christian: full speed ahead!"

"Yes, Sergeant D. Murphy," Christian mocked. He would have saluted if he weren't attempting to skillfully steer the canoe.

Soon they were beached. David secured the canoe to a tree before dashing for the cabin after Christian and Anna.

I hope whomever lives here is kind enough to let us stay 'till the storm is over, Anna thought.

136

"Think someone will be willing to take in three strangers?" David asked, echoing her thoughts.

"We're about to find out."

Christian reached up to knock on the door. When nobody answered, he pounded harder with his fist only to hear a loud thump followed by a groan coming from inside.

"Hello? Are you okay in there?" David asked, stepping up to the old wooden door beside Christian.

Unfortunately, the small overhang did little to shelter them from the downpour. A bolt of lightening and the ensuing clap of thunder seemed to fall directly behind them. "Man that was close!" David marveled, looking at the intensity of the storm. He pounded on the door. "Please, let us in before we get struck by lightening!" David couldn't wait any longer and turned the handle. The door slowly creaked open, and he tentatively glanced inside. A lone lamp lighted the room and a bed was against one wall in the cabin.

"What do you want?" came a weak and raspy, but familiar voice.

David opened the door wider and stepped in, soon followed by his cousins.

Dropping her backpack inside the door, Anna crossed to where the man lay next to his bed. Kneeing beside him she said, "Sir, we were just looking for a place to wait out the storm. Are you okay?"

"I'm fine. Now leave!" the man rasped, carefully pulling himself up to a standing position.

Anna jumped back, physically flinching as he towered over her. She suddenly realized why his voice had sounded so familiar. Slowly, she backed away from the old man and made her way toward Christian and David. Pointing to the man, she whispered, "That's the man who tried to scare me away!"

Before anyone could utter a word, the old man began coughing and collapsed to the floor. Christian and David ran to help the ailing man into a chair, realizing he was no longer a threat.

"I don't think he's in any position to scare anyone right now," David reassured Anna.

"My sister knows first-aid," Christian confidently volunteered

Anna's help.

Great! Anna thought, looking at Christian in disbelief.

The old man was too weak to argue, and still coughing, he nodded in reply.

Turning, Anna walked to the other end of the one room cabin that doubled as a kitchen. She rummaged around and found a tea-kettle. Filling it with water, she set it on the stove to boil. "David or Christian, would one of you please look for some tea?" Anna directed.

"Sure," David said and headed to the kitchen.

Anna marched back to the man. *If I weren't a Christian I'd leave right now. He really frightens me—even when he's sick he's intimidating!* The man's pained expression and lethargy caused Anna to feel somewhat sympathetic. After a brief hesitation she felt for his pulse. "Can you describe your symptoms?" she asked in concern, monitoring his heartbeat. It was weak but steady.

"I just have the flu," he answered tiredly.

Christian and Anna exchanged looks. Anna knew what he was thinking. *Not another person with the flu! Didn't Uncle Mike have to be hospitalized because of flu symptoms?*

Unaware of the conversation that had transpired, David returned carrying a cup with a tea bag and spoon already in it.

"Thanks," Anna said, giving David a warning glance as he handed the mug to her.

David looked puzzled until Christian leaned over to fill him in.

Anna squeezed the tea bag and removed the spoon before setting the cup in front of the man. She urged him to drink slowly.

After he had taken a few swallows, David said, "Look, his color is better; he looks flushed."

"He's feverish," Anna explained. "That's what's giving his cheeks the rosy color."

"Oh," David said, looking uncomfortably around the sparsely furnished room. "Um, do you think we could have some towels to dry off?"

"In the bathroom," the man slowly instructed, as if it pained him to talk.

David went to retrieve a towel. "Thanks."

Christian ventured, "Why did you try to scare Anna the other night in the woods?"

The old man grimaced. "The name's Bill Garrison. I was trying to scare you into leaving my home territory. I thought you were treasure seekers. I couldn't figure out why kids your age would be mixed up with that group. There use to be a man hiding from the law in these parts. But now I know that's not why you're here."

"How do you know that?" David asked suspiciously.

"Television. Your group found the half-ape half-man fossil. Not that I believe that kind of rubbish," he informed.

The Murphys exchanged looks, realizing they had made the news after all.

"That doesn't explain why you stole our tools and slashed our tents," David replied. His tone demanded an answer.

"The tools are over there in the corner. You boys can take them when you're ready to leave. I don't know anything about holes in your tent."

The teens didn't look convinced, but David replied, "They weren't holes; they were slash marks, like they were made with a knife."

"Nope, that wasn't me. I don't damage property. Sorry for scaring you," Bill apologized, "but like I said, I thought you were those thugs the sheriff's been after. I thought I had scared them away. It's been years since they've been around these parts."

Christian's eyes narrowed and he decided to take a wild guess, "That wouldn't be around the time when Hurricane Donna came through?" he asked. "Would it?"

Bill took another sip of tea before he answered. The strong flavor seemed to fortify him, "Well, now, come to think of it, it was about a month before the big storm. That man was a thief. He was real bad news. Rumor has it he would steal from other crooks! That's as low as you can get. Or so the rumor goes."

The Murphys listened in amazement as Bill continued. "They came and went, mostly working at night. They were using the river to transport their stolen loot. I did my best to scare them off and one day they up and left. I figured the FBI was getting too close or maybe, just maybe I had a hand in making them leave."

"What kinds of things did you do to scare them?" David asked, intrigued.

"I dressed up and pretended to be a wild bear." Bill laughed a low rumble and slightly coughed before clearing his throat to continue. "Yep, I spooked them a time or two."

Christian noticed the rain had stopped and the sky was clearing. "I think it's safe to continue our trip back to camp."

Looking around, Anna smiled, "Oh good; you have a phone. Do you mind if we give you a call this evening? If you don't answer then we'll know you need help."

"That's kind of you—the number is on the dial," Bill responded.

"Mind if we call our dad?" Anna queried.

"Sure, go ahead," Bill answered.

Having replaced the handset after speaking with her father and reassuring him of their safety, Anna thanked Mr. Garrison.

"Before we leave," Christian hesitated before finishing, "Do you mind if we pray for you?"

"Nope, not at all. I know Jesus is the best Physician a man can have."

Smiling, Christian and Anna began to pray. David stood wordlessly beside them, listening.

When they were through and still mindful of the moment, David asked in a hushed voice, "Are you sure it's wise to leave him here all by himself?"

"He may have been dehydrated," Anna quietly remarked to David, "but he should be okay now." Checking to see that there was a full pitcher of water nearby, Anna directed Mr. Garrison to drink plenty of fluids.

"Yes, thank-you, and sorry for the fright. Let your Dad know I thought you were someone else."

They quickly said their good-byes, and the three promised to call later that night and visit again soon.

Chapter 18
Missing Link, Lost!

Two days had passed since the encounter with the media and no further accusations had been made about who leaked the information. Deciding it futile to place the blame since the damage had already been done, Dr. Murphy let the issue drop. He knew more accusations would only cause more tension on the site. Although the understaffed sheriff's department was trying its best to patrol the area, a few reporters managed to sneak by, attempting to take pictures or ask questions.

Posting a sizable reward for any information leading to the whereabouts of his brother, Dr. Murphy saw an increase in leads coming into the sheriff's office. Many of them, however, turned out false. Since his offer to help the sheriff's department was declined, Dr. Murphy turned his full effort and attention toward the excavation. Everyone agreed that excavating Arcadia Man and much of the surrounding area should be completed as quickly as possible, and they all worked diligently toward that end. Taking breaks only for meals, sleep, and to attend church on Sunday, the teens somehow made time to visit old Bill Garrison who was making an amazing recovery.

Dr. Murphy invited Jim to join them for church and was dismayed that Jim had a hardened heart concerning such matters. Once professing his Christianity, Jim had left the faith. "It's not that I don't appreciate your offer to attend church," Jim had stated. "I respect your dedication to your belief system, Dr. Jack, but please respect my opinion. I've outgrown 'religion' and learned to rely on myself. I don't need God."

"Being a Christian doesn't mean you lose your personhood. Have you ever heard the Scripture verse... 'The truth will set you free'?" Dr. Murphy asked.

Jim didn't comment.

Dr. Murphy knew of many young people who had grown up attending church with their parents and upon leaving home became "enlightened" and rejected their faith. Some felt as Jim did that they no longer needed religion. Apparently, their Christian education lacked sufficient training to answer certain issues regarding science and the Bible. While no more was said about religion, Dr. Murphy felt the best evangelization tool for now was prayer and the example he could give by the way he lived his life.

Sitting back on his heels, Dr. Murphy wiped the sweat from his brow with a bandana before replacing his wide brimmed hat. "Well, it looks like we can see the light at the end of the tunnel."

"Yes, if you're indicating we're almost finished with the excavation, I agree," Jim stated. "The rain helped to loosen things up a bit."

Harry puffed as he pushed another heavy wheelbarrow of dirt down to the river. Due to the added moisture from the rain, the soil could not be sifted, and they were using the river and screens to strain the dirt. "I'm glad we're almost done, cause I'm looking forward to some time with the A/C!"

"Yeah, we're with you Harry!" Anna and Christian agreed.

"The humidity has soared," Dr. Murphy observed. "That's why it's so hot. From the way it feels, it's going to rain later on today," he warned.

David had been pensive all day, yet he diligently worked alongside his uncle and Jim. Concerned and saddened that his father couldn't be there for the finale, he nonetheless was glad it was over. "Uncle Jack, if we could get a board beneath the torso, I think we can lift him."

"Good suggestion, David. First I'd like to take a few shots. Anna, would you please bring me my camera? I want to get some close-up's of Arcadia Man." Carefully wiping his hands, Dr. Murphy ascertained there wasn't a trace of dirt on them before handling his expensive equipment.

Anna had already taken some pictures, but her father's experience far outweighed her own. *Will I ever be half as good a photographer?* she wondered as she watched him focus and take shots from several angles. Never failing to amaze, Dr. Murphy worked quickly and accurately. Anna was certain his pictures would be spectacular in print.

"Here you go, Honey. Thanks."

Replacing the camera in its case, Anna noticed the wind had picked up. "Dad, it looks like the rain is going to be coming sooner than you thought."

David looked up at the sky. "The storm came quickly a few days ago and caught us by surprise, Uncle Jack," he declared, standing beside the fossil.

A bolt of lightening streaked through the sky followed by a terrific clap of thunder. "It may be a good idea to cover up Arcadia Man and wait until this storm passes over," Dr. Murphy suggested to Jim.

"No!" Jim almost shouted. Taking a controlled breath he calmly finished. "This needs to be completed. Now. Having to stop because of the storms the last few days has cost us valuable time, especially yester—" A horrific clap of thunder drowned out the remainder of his words. He instinctively bent down and covered his head.

"Yesterday's rain was heavy, but over quickly," Dr. Murphy reminded him. "You know that Florida lightening storms are nothing to ignore. We should seek cover."

"Let's get the yellow pine brace under Arcadia Man. Then if the storm is severe, we can stop," Jim insisted.

Against his better judgment, Dr. Murphy agreed. "Fine, bring the wood over, Harry, and we'll do it."

143

As the winds picked up, bits of sand and debris were blown around the campsite. Lightening zigzagged across the sky and peals of thunder sounded as Anna and Christian scurried around the site gathering as many objects as they could and placing them in the tent. Large pelts of rain began to fall.

"Use the flat edge of your shovel to leverage the torso while I place the two-by-four under him," Dr. Murphy directed. Using his weight, Dr. Murphy wedged a piece of wood underneath.

"Be careful!" Jim screamed. "We don't want to damage him!"

"No, we don't." Dr. Murphy gritted his teeth as he puffed from the exertion. Water beaded on his face. "David, use that trowel to scoop some more dirt out from underneath. I can't seem to get the board straight—something must be blocking it!"

Nodding, David dropped on all fours and dug as much as he could. Valiantly straining, Jim and Harry used their shovels to hold up Arcadia Man at an angle, which turned out to be no small feat. Encased in dirt, the fossilized remains weighed well over several hundred pounds.

Dr. Murphy pushed and shoved, finally securing the board underneath. "There!" he exclaimed as he stood back and proudly viewed their work.

As if on cue, thunder blasted and the heavens opened as a torrential downpour began. Grabbing the protective tarp, which had been moved earlier to enable moving freely around the remains, they attempted to cover the fossil. The winds made it difficult to secure.

"Grab the other side!" Jim screeched. "Come on, David! What are you doing? Harry! Come-on, man! Help!"

"I'm working; what are you doing?" David yelled back over the howling wind. Harry grabbed the opposite end of the tarp, pulling tightly. David inadvertently let go of his end, which sent Harry tumbling back—taking the tarp with him. Making a wild grab, Dr. Murphy missed and stood watching in dismay as Harry slid down the slippery embankment and toward the river's edge.

"Hey!" Jim yelled racing after Harry. He wanted to retrieve the tarp more than to help.

Having secured the area, Christian and Anna stood high and

dry under the tent canopy watching the antics and chuckling. David turned at the sound of laughter. Smiling, he climbed out of Arcadia Man's pit and went to join them.

Anna took in David's mud-caked appearance and handed him a towel. "It's going to take more than this towel to get you clean," she claimed, laughing.

"At least we're done, though!" David said, taking the towel and wiping his face. "This rain will naturally wash off the dirt and sand caked onto the fossil, so I don't know why Jim was so bent on getting him covered. Now all we have to do is brace the remains and call in a chopper to air lift him out of here. I really wish dad were here to see this," David added wistfully.

Placing a reassuring hand on her cousin's arm, Anna softly replied, "I know, David. So do we." For once he didn't shake it off.

Together the teens watched as Dr. Murphy, Jim, and Harry climbed up the embankment. They had given up on covering the fossil. Just as they reached the top, Jim screeched. "Stop him! Somebody! Do something!"

From the effects of pelting rain, the remainder of dirt around Arcadia Man had quickly eroded. The wooden planks that lifted the fossil out of the pit also allowed the rain to do in minutes what had taken them days to do by hand.

Running out from the shelter and ignoring the rain, the three watched in shock as Arcadia Man slid down the embankment on the plank of wood and right into the Peace River!

Chapter 19
The Missing Link

Standing in shocked silence for what seemed like hours, the group watched as the river gently lapped the fossil lying on the shoreline. With the rain abated, the remaining drizzle perfectly matched their mood.

Dr. Murphy, the first to snap out of his shocked disbelief, suggested they pray.

"Now? At a time like this?" Jim shouted.

Ignoring him, Dr. Murphy quickly bowed his head and asked the Lord's help in the matter. During the prayer, David broke into the circle and joined hands with them. Anna and Christian, with bowed heads, exchanged looks and smiled.

"Okay. Now let's get busy," Dr. Murphy quietly instructed the group with authority. Each was given a job, and they all gathered their tools and met at the water's edge.

Upon closer inspection, Dr. Murphy noted the fossil, now lying face down, had suffered a crack along its side, although it remained intact. Squatting down at the river's edge, he looked up at the small group gathered in a semi-circle around him and commented, "We have our work cut out for us."

"It's ruined—it's ruined!" Jim wailed.

"We don't know if the crack was preexisting or a result of the fall," Dr. Murphy calmly reminded. "Jim, get a grip on yourself," he urged, "or you won't be of any help."

Jim sighed and looked at Dr. Murphy. "How can you be so calm, Dr. Jack?"

"I'm working under the power of God's grace and He is sustaining me," Dr. Murphy replied. If I was relying on my own strength I'd be distraught like you."

Jim seemed not to hear. "My reputation as a world class paleoanthropologist was going to be made with this find," he fretted, waving his arms for emphasis. "My name would go down in the history books as excavator of the first entirely intact, positively identified transitional fossil. A definite ape-like creature-to-man link! Now look at it. It's stuck in the mud underwater!"

"Correction!" Dr. Murphy interjected. "It's just on the water's edge and if we hurry before the river swells from rain, it won't sink any further," he claimed, disappointed with Jim for putting his needs above everything else. "Arcadia Man is not yet lost, but I'm of half a mind to push him the remainder of the way into the river and let him sink to the bottom!"

He wouldn't! Anna thought in shock as she looked at her father's stormy features. Standing with his hands on hips and glaring at Jim, she knew he was angry. But her father's words were just what Jim needed to hear.

"What? Dr. Jack!" Jim snapped back to reality. "Please don't do it! Come on, everyone—let's help."

"I thought you would change your mind," Dr. Murphy muttered half under his breath.

Christian, Anna, and David were ready with shovels in hand. "Where's Harry?" Jim inquired.

"He went into the tent for something. I guess he'll be here soon," David answered.

"Here I am," announced Harry, puffing as he half slid, half walked down the slippery slope toward the group. He carried rope and a tarp to cover the fossil once they had it ready to transport, just as he had been directed earlier.

Quickly organizing the group, Dr. Murphy laid out a plan. Using the remaining two-by-fours as leverage, they would lift Arcadia Man high enough to place wooden planks underneath him. Once this was done, they would lower him onto additional two-by-fours running perpendicular to the boards already in position. They would then brace him and call for a chopper to airlift him out. "Maybe we should call the helicopter now," Dr. Murphy suggested, thinking aloud. "By the time we get this ready to airlift, it could be here."

"Good idea—I'll call," Harry said, bolting for the tent and his cell phone. "I know one of the locals who should be able to come."

"Thanks," Dr. Murphy responded. "Okay crew, let's go."

Harry quickly rejoined them and after a vigorous hour of digging, they finally made some progress. Although the position of the sun now peeking through the clouds indicated lunchtime, no one mentioned food. In time, enough dirt was removed to place the wood underneath the fossil which still lay face down. Christian, David, Anna, and Harry stood knee-deep in the water with strips of two-by-fours under the fossil and pushed down as directed.

Occasionally Anna glanced nervously in the water behind her, looking for tell-tale signs of movement.

"Don't worry," Christian encouraged, observing her apprehension, "the gators are far away." He said it with more conviction than he felt.

Anna nodded agreement. "I hope you're right."

"Hold it!" Jim suddenly shouted. "Careful now! Easy does it," he directed nervously. "We want to turn him gently and minimize the damage. Understand people?"

"Just be ready to catch him at your end when we flip him over," David said through clenched teeth, straining under the weight.

Dr. Murphy directed the four to put their weight on the wood after he had wedged in pieces of pine to use as fulcrums. "Okay. Now lean down hard!" he instructed.

Grunting filled the air as the four placed all of their weight on the wood. The fossilized remains slowly lifted from its muddy perch and rolled over onto the two-by- fours with a thud.

"It worked like a charm!" Jim shouted. "What luck!"

149

"No luck about it," Christian answered. "It seems to me we had some Divine help!"

"Agreed!" Anna stated, looking at her Dad with a smile. He winked back in response.

"Now what, Uncle Jack? How are you planning to airlift him from here?" David asked, still worried about the position of Arcadia Man so close to the river's edge.

"We are now going to secure him with tarps and rope. With the use of steel cables, the helicopter will hopefully lift him out to safety. Your father had already planned for this and we have the necessary supplies.

"I wish he were here now," David said voicing the consensus of the group.

"So do I," Dr. Murphy replied, walking toward his nephew. He placed a reassuring arm around his shoulder and pulled him into a tight hug.

A somber mood fell over the group with the realization the work was completed. The wrapping of Arcadia Man under Jim's careful and urgent supervision was accomplished in record time.

"Okay, kids, move it now. Go on! We have important work to complete here," Jim dictated. "David, why don't you kids begin by breaking down some of the camp—but stay out of my specimen tent!" he ordered.

"It's irritating the way he thinks this is his find!" Anna whispered as she and Christian moved aside, allowing Jim to pass. Exhausted, they followed David up the incline to the camp.

"You heard him," Christian whispered back. "This is going to bring him fame and fortune. He probably will be interviewed and featured in various types of journals like the *National Geographic* and *Nature*, to say nothing of nightly television news shows."

Anna stopped from time to time to take pictures of the group, raising her voice once they were out of earshot. "Yeah, you're probably right. Would you believe he's already asked me for copies of all my pictures?"

"He'll probably sell them to magazines," Christian said uncharitably, "and keep the money for himself. The worst part about all

150

this is Uncle Mike isn't around to get any of the publicity or prestige from the find that was originally his."

"Even though he'd be getting honor for a fossil we still don't think is actually the missing link?" Anna asked.

"Yeah well, that goes without saying," Christian remarked.

"Isn't it convenient that Uncle Mike is out of the picture," Anna concluded once they reached the landing.

"What do you mean?"

"Well, isn't it a coincidence Jim should get all the glory that rightly belongs to Uncle Mike?"

"Well…"

"And," Anna interrupted, "Isn't it amazing how Uncle Mike is the only one to come down with the flu, which then turned to pneumonia? How come no one else got sick?"

"You're not saying that Jim is involved in the kidnapping and in getting Uncle Mike sick!" Christian hooted with laughter. He made sure to lower his voice when the others looked over at them. "The doctors said it was some type of virus. What did he do, inject Uncle Mike?"

"How do I know? I'm not an expert on germ warfare," Anna scowled, angry with her brother for making fun of her. "How about putting something in his drink? Could that be possible?"

"Maybe, but I think your imagination is running wild again," Christian cautioned as he played with the idea. Far out as it might seem, it did appear that their uncle had been removed for a reason.

"Up until now, there appears to be no evidence and no motive for Uncle Mike's disappearance. There must be a reason, and if the only person I can think of is Jim having a motive, than that's better than nothing," Anna huffed. "Perhaps we should let David in on our— or should I say, my—suspicions?" Anna felt hurt that Christian didn't concur with her line of reasoning.

"Wait a minute," Christian cautioned. "Before we jump to conclusions, we should consider the implications. Wouldn't it be horrible to blame someone and then discover we were wrong?"

"Yes, but the evidence does point to Jim," Anna stubbornly reminded him. "Anyway, I'm only stating facts. Jim is here. Uncle

Mike is missing—and no one knows where."

"Don't forget Lauren and the man in the boat, Mr. SUV. They're somehow mixed up in something perhaps related to this excavation." Looking at Anna's stormy face, Christian relented, sighing, "Okay, I admit we can't overlook the fact that Jim is focused on the fame aspect of this dig more than anything else. We can question him, or search his things to look for something that can link him to our suspicions."

Hearing him say "our" suspicions went a long way toward mollifying Anna. "Okay, Christian, thanks. But, I'm not sure I like the idea of you searching his tent."

The roar of the approaching helicopter put an end to their discussion. Quickly readying her camera, Anna set it on automatic for the shots she would take as Arcadia Man was airlifted.

Hovering above river, the helicopter positioned itself as Dr. Murphy and Jim waited for the cable with canvas to be lowered. The apparatus consisted of two large thick canvas strips. One side had three metal hooks that were stationary, while the other side had one removable hook. Since the fossil lay on planks of wood, they would need to place the canvas beneath the wood to lift him.

"Jim, go ahead and unhook the ends and feed the canvas under. I'll fish it out from this side," Dr. Murphy instructed. He knelt in the mud, looking under Arcadia Man, as Jim shoved the canvas as far as his hands could reach.

"I hope they realize how important this package is," Jim said laughing, almost giddy with excitement. His dreams were about to be realized.

"I've got it—I think. Push a little more…"

"How's that?" Jim asked.

"Great! Yes, here it comes," Dr. Murphy replied, pulling the canvas under the fossil and beginning to place the hooks through the metal-riveted holes.

"Wait! Let me do that," Jim ordered, grabbing the cable out of Dr. Murphy's grip, none too gently. "I don't want to take the chance of anything happening to my discovery." Jim made no effort to hide any pretense that all this was a shared effort.

"Yours?" Dr. Murphy asked raising his eyebrow in disbelief. However, his question went unanswered. Standing back, he watched as Jim hooked the cables and gave the signal for the pilot to begin his ascent.

Slowly lifting the canvas-wrapped Arcadia Man, the helicopter hovered several inches above the ground. The weight from the heavy fossil pulled the cables taunt.

"Anna, I'm glad you're getting pictures of this," David commented as he came and stood beside his cousin. "I'll want to show them to Dad."

Anna paused to give her cousin a quick, but worried glance. "I'm trying to capture every stage," she answered looking though the lenses once more, fascinated with the procedure.

The helicopter slowly rose as it continued to check the balance of weight. The engines roared and the pilot readied to pick up speed.

Twang! Twang! The strange sound heard over the roaring blades came from the vicinity of the chopper. The small group looked around, puzzled—each trying to place the strange noise.

"Oh no!" Anna screamed while pointing. Suddenly it was evident that one hook had come undone and now dangled uselessly. Arcadia Man began to slide off the sling. They watched in helpless horror as the fossilized remains of the only intact missing link tipped precariously toward the river!

Chapter 20
X Marks the Spot

"Grab it! Quickly! Jim screamed as he raced to save the fossil. He stood directly under the hovering helicopter with hands outstretched.

"Get back!" Dr. Murphy yelled, immediately tackling Jim and knocking him out of the way.

When the experienced helicopter pilot felt the load shift in weight, he rapidly lowered the cargo. It landed where Jim had been standing moments earlier. If Dr. Murphy had not intervened, Jim would have been crushed.

"Jim! Are you insane? You could have been killed!" Dr. Murphy shouted as he rubbed his leg. While attempting to save Jim, Dr. Murphy landed on a rock and was certain his leg would be sporting a bruise to show for it.

Jim remained where he had fallen, reality settling in. He didn't say a word as he watched Dr. Murphy brush himself off and walk over to re-clamp the hook through the metal ring on Arcadia Man.

Briefly inspecting the remaining hooks and rings, Dr. Murphy double-checked the cargo before he gave a thumbs-up signal for the pilot to head out. Once again the helicopter hovered. Discerning that the weight was now evenly distributed and secure, it began to slowly rise.

Anna held her breath as she watched the helicopter successfully hover this time, gain speed, and fly away. "Whew!" she exhaled, "That was close!" She was happy for this phase of the excavation to be over.

"Man! What a rush!" David shouted, taking off his hat and waving it at the departing 'copter. "I can't wait to see those pictures! It's as if some invisible hand was holding him up," David claimed, grinning sheepishly at the looks on his cousins' faces.

Anna and Christian exchanged looks and laughed.

"Great, now I'm starting to sound like you guys!"

"Seriously though, you're right; it does appear to be a miracle," Christian agreed. He sobered at the thought. *Perhaps God really wants man to know more about evolution and therefore wanted the evidence preserved.* The thought lasted only a split-second before he quickly rejected it. *More like He wants His creation evidenced by this!*

"Maybe the Lord wants Arcadia Man to remain intact to prove he's not the missing link," Anna said, confirming Christian's thoughts. "If he had fallen into the river and broken in pieces, perhaps parts of him would have been gone. Then the proof would have been lost for both sides."

Dr. Murphy was talking to a still somber Jim as they climbed the short distance to the top of the hill. "Seriously, Jim, not many people are given a second chance at life. You should take this as a gift from God. Do you realize you could have been fatally injured?"

Jim nodded his head in bewilderment and silently walked toward the tent to clean up, change, and retrieve his things.

He doesn't look good, Anna thought, watching the disheveled man shuffle slowly along. *I should talk to Dad.*

Dr. Murphy agreed with Anna that Jim needed help overseeing the remaining details of the trip and planned to accompany him to the local airport. Arcadia Man was to be transported in the cargo section of a private charter flight and the arrangements would need to be verified before the fossil headed to a Texas lab.

Having made all the arrangements months prior, Mike's

efficiency was evident when a quick call to the lab assured that the scientists were still expecting Arcadia Man.

"I'll return later in the day help tear this site down and clean up," Dr. Murphy informed. He and Jim left soon afterward.

It wasn't long before David set down the plastic trash bag forcefully and flounced into a chair. "After three hours we're still not finished!" he complained. "I can't believe Jim left and we're stuck with all the cleaning! He gets the honors; we get the mess!"

"We're almost through," Christian pointed out while on one knee to pull up another tent stake.

Anna inwardly sighed, *David has come such a long way, but I guess I still need to pray!*

"We've been 'almost' done for the past hour!" David complained with exasperation as he wiped the sweat from his face with the back of his hand. It left a big streak of dirt. Surveying the area, he noted most of the tents had been dismantled, tools stacked, and personal belongings packed. "There's still the specimen tent that has to wait for your dad's return. Did you forget that?" David asked sighing.

"No we didn't," Anna said, working at the easy task of packing her father's photography equipment. Being meticulous, he always returned an object to its place as soon as possible. "I have an idea," Anna suggested brightly, "When we're through, let's hop in the canoe and visit Bill. I wonder how he's doing." Anna hoped they would have time.

"Sounds good to me—that is, if we ever get done!" David grumbled, although he was somewhat mollified.

"On second thought, maybe we should clean ourselves before we go anywhere," she stated, pointing at the boys and giggling. "You two are a mess!"

"It's a good thing you can't see yourself," David howled with laughter. The boys looked down at their partially dry clothing, shoes caked in dirt, and mud-stained faces.

"Yep, we sho' are a sight, that's fer sho'!" Christian said doing his best to imitate a southern accent. A ringing cell phone caught

157

their attention.

"I've got it," Anna responded. When the call concluded she quickly updated the boys. "Dad said he's been delayed. Somehow newspaper reporters, television crews, and even a journalist from a national magazine were at the airport waiting! According to dad, it was bedlam. The media has been demanding information about Arcadia Man. Can you believe that?" Anna asked in disgust. "I wonder how they found out."

"I can only guess," Christian said as they exchanged knowing looks. The unspoken name, Jim, was on all their minds.

"How about if you guys finish up here?" Anna asked. Pushing her hair out of her eyes and trying not to get dirt on the only part of her that was clean, she added, "I can start in the specimen tent. It's a big mess with all those papers and samples."

"Shouldn't you leave it for Dad?" Christian asked.

"I'll leave the specimens for him to sort through, but for some reason it looks like a hurricane went through that tent and if someone doesn't start the job of tidying up in there, we'll be here another week—at least!"

"Suit yourself," David responded. "I for one don't want to tackle that job. Dad would never have tolerated that mess; he's always organized and insists on carefully logging every detail."

"Alright, I'll get right on it." Looking from Christian to David, Anna began walking toward the tent and then paused. "Are either of you going to work?"

Both boys nodded in the affirmative, but neither moved. David sat slumped in a chair, and Christian leaned against a tree. Harry had long since given up helping. He was now in his tent, one of the few still standing, and making another call.

Anna shrugged her shoulders in resignation. She walked into the research tent and grimaced. *Man, is it ever a mess in here!* With a makeshift table in the center piled high with papers, scribbled notes, and journal entries, it was an organizational nightmare. She quickly stacked papers into neat piles and debated placing them into crates. Grabbing one, she decided to start on the side of the tent where a stack of quart-size resealable bags lay in a pile. All were neatly labeled with specific descriptions of where the contents were discovered. Each bag also contained a number that corresponded to a waterproof notebook containing detailed information. *This looks like David's writing,* Anna thought as she read some of the entries. Smiling to herself, she absently placed most of the bags in the crate without a thought. Suddenly, Anna noted a bag that caught her eye. It wasn't transparent like the other bags, yet it was labeled. Anna opened the bag and looked in, careful not to touch the sample as she turned it over. The bag contained a piece of what appeared to be fossilized rock with an imbedded penny. She squinted at the penny and read the date, *1967. That's odd...what's this doing in here?* she wondered.

Meanwhile, Christian pushed away from the tree and asked, "Did anyone pick up the tools that were used in the excavation?" He pointed in the direction where Arcadia Man lay only hours earlier.

"Aw, man! Not there! It was a mess the last time I looked," David groaned, violently shaking his head. Still sitting, he buried his head in his hands.

"Come on, David, the sooner we get moving, the sooner we'll be done," Christian prodded. Not waiting for his cousin, he headed down the slippery incline.

David finally decided to follow. "You know, if this were South Africa or Egypt, we could easily have hired locals to help with the cleanup. They would be happy for the work, and I would be happy not doing it!"

"Really? That would've been great," Christian agreed.

The ground was still slick and muddy from the recent rain. David opened his mouth to caution about the slippery ground just as Christian lost his footing and slid partially down the embankment.

Grabbing unsuccessfully for a handhold, Christian tumbled into the hole where Arcadia Man lay hours before. "Yeow!" he shouted as his right knee collided with a sharp object and began to bleed.

David swallowed a chuckle at the scene of a muddy Christian becoming muddier still. "Are you okay?" he asked, sliding down to help.

"Yeah I just...hey, David, look at this!" yelled Christian excitedly as he pushed himself up.

David, cautious not to slip at the same place Christian did, gingerly picked his way to Christian's side. He now stood in the water that hours of rain left as a deposit.

"This better be worth it. My shoes are getting wet again," David complained.

"Get a load of this!" Christian exclaimed and stepped back so David had a better view of the object.

"So? It looks like the corner of a rusty metal box. Big deal," David said with disappointment. "Hey, wait a minute! This is in the same strata as Arcadia man—and would somehow be linked to the fossil!"

"Wow! You're right!" Christian exclaimed. "Anna, come here, quick!" he called over his shoulder. "And bring a big shovel!"

Startled by the urgency in Christian's voice, Anna rushed out of the research tent and pocketed the baggie without much thought. She ran over to the top of the embankment and looked down. "What is it, Christian? Hey! What are you guys doing? You're supposed to be cleaning up!"

"Bring some shovels and hurry!"

"There are plenty of trowels down there. Why do you want a shovel?"

"Come-on Anna, I found something here," Christian explained.

"Oh, alright!" Anna shouted as she walked to the where the storage tent once stood. She pulled a large pointed shovel out of a box that had been packed and ready to load into the boat. *I wonder what Harry's up to! At least one load of this stuff should have already been transported to the marina,* she thought.

Hearing the commotion, Harry hastily rushed out of his tent and over to where the boys were.

Anna carefully made her way to where David stood, halfway up the embankment. Handing him several shovels, she asked, "What's going on?"

"Come see what I found!" Christian shouted excitedly. "Careful though, it's a nasty fall and I've got the bruised knee to prove it."

"That area's off limits, son," Harry stated flatly.

"We'll be careful," David said. "I've had lots of years

160

of experience."

"Look at this, Harry!" Christian exclaimed as he showed him the partially exposed metal box.

"Let's dig it up!" Anna encouraged, sliding into the crevice beside the boys. She grabbed one of the shovels and began to carefully scrape away the mud.

A strange expression crossed Harry's face. "I'll be right back." The three adventurers were too eager and busy to notice Harry's absence. While carefully checking the area for other fossilized remains, they dug around the box and placed the dirt into ever-present plastic buckets. Their excitement mounted as more and more of the large box became exposed.

"We could be digging up treasure!" Anna said after several minutes of silence.

"Or it could just be something some kids buried a long time ago for fun," David commented, heaving another shovel full of mud.

"We won't know until we dig it out," Anna replied.

The water made work difficult as the sides of the pit continued to cave in. "We have a bilge pump, but I for one am too tired to get it, haul it down here, and fire it up," David admitted.

"We may need it if we can't get the box loose," Christian explained, "But I agree. Let's not use the pump unless absolutely necessary."

The box was extremely heavy and wedged in the mud so it wouldn't budge. "The surrounding area doesn't appear to be fossilized," David noted.

"You're right," Christian said, "Let's keep digging until the majority of the rusted box is exposed. Then we can try to lift it."

A short time later, the metal box was ready to be moved. Staking his shovel in the dirt above the hole, David suggested, "Okay on the count of three we'll try lifting it."

Christian took one side and David the other. "When we lift it up, you put the piece of two-by-four underneath. Okay, Anna?"

"Got it!" she said picking up the wood. *This is too strange! I feel like we're working with Arcadia man all over again.*

"Okay. One, two, and three!" Christian shouted.

161

"Lift!" Anna cried as she shoved the wood under the rusty object.

The huge box crept up only a few inches from the mucky ground, but it was enough for Anna to slide the wood underneath.

"Man! That thing has to weigh at least 200 pounds!" David exclaimed after setting his end down on the two-by-four.

"Forget about how much it weighs. Let's see what's in it!" Anna said.

"I think we should get it out of here first."

"Good idea," Christian agreed, although he too was impatient to see the contents.

"I'll get some rope. That'll be the easiest way to get it out," David claimed, lifting himself out of the hole.

"I'm one step ahead of you," Harry announced, coming back into view. "I figured you'd need rope. Have you opened the box yet?" he calmly inquired.

"No, we figured we'd pull it up first," Christian said. *Man! Where have you been while we've been doing all the hard work?* Christian secretly wondered. *Now I'm beginning to sound like David!*

"The handles are rusted and won't hold the weight of the box," David informed. "But tying the rope around the bottom will give us a better chance," he suggested, jumping back into the hole.

After securing the rope around the bottom, the four yanked with all their might. They strained and grunted, only to sigh with exhaustion upon noticing the box had barely budged.

"Christian, why don't you get back into the pit and push while we tug?" David asked.

"Sounds good to me," Christian said, doing as directed.

The four were delighted to see the box slowly inch out of the hole. They pushed and pulled until it landed upon a small area of level ground near the camp.

Anna laughed. "If we thought we were dirty before, you should see us now! We look like mud people!"

"Who cares!" Harry shouted with delight. He was as excited as they were. Slicing the ropes with a pocketknife, his attempt to

162

open the box was fruitless.

"This box looks fairly recent," David remarked. "Does anyone know how to pick a lock?" he asked in dismay, pointing to the padlock.

Christian bent down to get a better look. He pulled and rattled the lock. Trying to lift the lid, he noticed the rear hinges were loose and the box could be opened about a quarter of an inch.

"We need a way to finish breaking the lock," David said.

"Stand back," Christian ordered, retrieving his shovel.

"Wait!" Anna shouted. "What if this is an important artifact and we're breaking the lock? Shouldn't we wait until Dad comes back?"

David looked at the lock. "The box is already damaged, and I doubt it has any value. The lock looks fairly recent. I say go for it, Christian!"

Needing no further encouragement, Christian accurately aimed and swung the shovel like a baseball bat. Whack! He hit the lock squarely in the middle. A crunching of metal and a thud resulted. The rusted lock fell onto the muddy ground.

"Open it, quick!"

"What's in it?"

All three teens knelt down with Harry hovering close behind. Christian pushed the lid back and they all gazed in stunned silence—astonished at the contents.

"Now, isn't that strange?" Harry said, puzzled.

"It can't be!" Christian said with disgust.

"All this work for nothing?" David asked.

"The entire box is full of mud!" Christian exclaimed, "No wonder it was so heavy."

"Wait a minute!" Anna urged, peering into it intently. "Look!" She picked up a stick and stuck it into the box. It pierced the mud several inches and then stopped. She stuck her hand in and began pushing away the layer of muck.

Christian helped Anna shovel the mud out with his hands, too. After digging out several inches of mud, they encountered the bottom. Christian announced, "This box appears empty, but it's much deeper than it looks."

"Maybe it has a false bottom," David answered. "I've seen this before! Let me borrow your pocketknife."

Handing his knife to David, Christian moved out of the way.

Slowly David inched the sharp point around the perimeter of the box. Finding a tiny hole, he placed the blade tip into it and pried gently. The cover of the false bottom sprang open. There, sparkling in the sun, was a compartment full of gold coins!

Chapter 21
Who To Trust?

The three looked at the treasure in amazement. Grabbing a handful of coins, David let them trickle through his fingers and fall back into the box. Harry immediately took several steps back. They were mesmerized by sparkling treasure and totally taken aback when Harry took several steps forward, pointed a gun at them and snarled, "Put your hands where I can see them and get away from that chest!"

Startled, all three whirled around and Christian made a move to stand up.

"Don't try anything," Harry warned, waving his gun in front of them for emphasis.

Not wanting to take any chances, Anna and Christian stepped away from the treasure chest and turned to face him.

Still kneeling, David scowled, "What are you doing, Harry?"

"What do you think? I'm going to be rich!" he scoffed.

"Do you know what these coins are?" David asked haughtily.

Anna bit her lip, knowing his comments would only get them into more trouble. Christian shook his head, silently pleading with David not to say anything more.

"Yeah, gold coins," Harry answered sarcastically. "Now be quiet so I can think," he finished.

Pretending to ignore him, David picked up one of the coins and looked at it critically. "They look like Spanish doubloons to me. The only way you're going to be able to sell them without anybody tracing it back to you is on the Black Market," David explained. "See? You need to think this through. It's not going to be as easy as you imagined."

Still pointing the gun, Harry looked confused for a moment and then brightened. "I'll just take you with me."

"No!—You can't!" David protested in alarm, quickly standing and taking a step back.

"Who's gonna stop me?" Harry laughed. "You're the one who seems to know so much about these coins, telling me how valuable they are. Besides you'll come in handy as a hostage."

Oh great; David's plan backfired! Instead of convincing Harry the coins would be impossible to sell without connections, he just gave Harry a reason to kidnap him—or maybe worse! Christian thought, glancing at his sister to signal he was attempting an escape.

Seeing her brother was planning something, Anna shook her head to warn Christian, but he didn't seemed to notice.

If David can keep Harry busy, maybe I can jump him, Christian thought while sizing Harry up. He knew it would be risky. Harry outweighed him by at least sixty pounds and had the added advantage of a loaded weapon.

"David, take that rope and tie up your kin," Harry demanded, indicating the rope they recently used to haul up the gold.

When David hesitated, Harry walked toward him and pointed the pistol directly at his head. "Now!" he shouted. David sprang into action and reached for the rope.

"Tie 'em to that tree," Harry gestured with the tip of his pistol.

"Christian, Anna…I—"

Harry cut him off. "No talking!" He roared. "I don't have much time!"

"I'm sorry," David mouthed as he tied up his two cousins. He tied each of their wrists together and then around the tree. Harry kept a watchful eye on them.

"Put the coins in here," Harry ordered as he threw several large bags at David.

Prolonging the task as much as possible, David secretly hoped his uncle would return. With each passing second, however, Harry's foul temper worsened.

"You think I don't know what you're doing, Kid? Your Uncle is gonna be back any minute, and if he does show up before we leave, I'll shoot you all! Now hurry up and put those bags in the boat!"

He's not kidding, David. Do what he says, Anna silently urged as she observed Harry's round face redden with rage.

Seeing it wasn't an idle threat, David lugged the heavy canvas bag of gold coins toward the waiting boat. "I'm hurrying! Just don't hurt my cousins!"

Harry lumbered over to Christian and Anna to check the ropes. Pulling at the binds, he discovered they were extremely loose. "I can't have you getting away and following us," he huffed in irritation. "You kids are sure trying my patience."

"You won't get away with this," Christian warned.

Harry bellowed with laughter as he secured the ropes so they were unbearably tight. " 'Course I will! Who's gonna stop me? Sheriff Simons or his deputies? Heck, I've grown up with half of 'em and can whoop 'em all!"

"There's one thing you can be sure of, Harry," Anna informed. "Truth has a way of catching up with people. You can't hide forever."

"Now that, little missy, is for you to ponder and for me to find out," Harry harshly laughed. "There! I'm finished. And by the way, I'm taking your phone."

Great. Now we can't even call for help! Anna frowned in dismay.

"Come on, David, move it!" Harry snarled.

David lugged the remaining bags of gold to the boat while Harry followed close behind.

Anna and Christian heard the motor sputter several times before roaring to life. Quickly the sound faded away as Harry and David made their way up river.

"Now what?" Anna asked, wiggling her nearly numb fingers.

"We're stranded and without a car, a boat, or a phone!"

"Not necessarily. Can you reach your hand into my pocket and get my knife?" Christian asked. He scooted over and Anna tried to reach.

"It's no use! I can't feel my fingers," she exclaimed fearfully and leaned her head back against the tree.

"Close your eyes, Anna," Christian consoled, recognizing the panic in her voice.

Anna was puzzled but did what Christian asked. She squeezed her eyes tightly.

Christian began to pray. "Dear Lord, we need you in a mighty way. We might never see David or Uncle Mike again without Your help. Please help us out of this situation, give us peace, and guide us. Please, Lord, we need a miracle! In Jesus' name we pray," Christian finished. "Amen," they closed in unison.

"Thanks, I feel better."

"Now, if we could just get a message to Dad or the sheriff, we'd be set," Christian stated, wiggling and pulling with all his might. His efforts were of no avail and only resulted in chafing his wrists. Five minutes grew to ten until they lost track of all time. Each felt dejected and wished things had turned out differently.

"Finding treasure buried beneath Arcadia Man sure sheds a new light on this mystery," Christian remarked, breaking the silence. He had been mulling over the facts.

"Now it makes sense why someone wanted Uncle Mike out of the way," Anna responded in agreement.

"Maybe they thought with him out of the way the dig would stop," Christian shook his head. "They obviously never met Jim."

"I wonder if Harry was part of the group that took Uncle Mike," Anna mused.

"It makes sense, since he could keep an eye on what was happening and report back," Christian said. "I wonder if they knew gold was buried here. And do you think there's any connection between Harry and Lauren? Remember the day we saw them in town?

Anna hung her head. "Yes, but this all sounds so sinister. To think someone might have been watching us the whole time!"

"What's that noise?" Christian suddenly asked.

"What?"

"Listen! Do you hear that? It sounds like a motorboat approaching," he brightened.

"Could Harry be coming back? Or is it Dad?" Anna asked.

"I don't know, but it sounds like it's going really fast," Christian related.

As the boat drew near and motor shut off, they decided to take a chance and began yelling as loudly as they could.

"Help! Hey—Over here!"

Watching, they saw a single figure climb the riverbank. Each prayed it would be anyone but Harry. Through the vegetation, a large man emerged.

"Bill! Help us!" Anna and Christian called in unison.

"What's he doing here?" Christian hissed, "You don't think he's part of Harry's group?

"I doubt it, Christian! Remember? He's the one that wanted us gone."

"Yeah, but maybe because he knew the treasure existed," Christian informed. "He wanted us out of the way so he could dig it up."

Anna gasped as Bill approached them and brandished the blade of his pocketknife. *Is this the end?*

"Are you kids alright? What happened?" Bill asked while sawing through the ropes.

"It's a long story, but one of the excavators, Harry Bradley, kidnapped David and stole some gold coins we uncovered," Anna summarized as best she could. She rubbed her sore wrists and eyed him carefully, looking for any reaction that might indicate his possible involvement. Anna was glad to see his surprise.

"Gold!" Bill shook his head, "I suppose it wouldn't take much to make Harry turn bad."

"He and David headed upriver," Christian added quickly, anxious to follow after them.

"I just passed them about ten minutes ago." Bill brightened, nodding his head toward the river.

"Did he see you?" Anna gasped.

"Come to think of it, he did, but didn't wave back," Bill mused. "Is there anyway I can help?"

"Can we borrow your boat?" Christian pleaded.

"No," he stated without ceremony, "but I'll take you. I know this river well and can get us there quickly." Bill's long strides were already heading toward the river.

"Are you sure you feel up to it?" Anna asked, hurrying to keep up with him. Christian was just steps behind.

"I'm feeling wonderful," he reassured. "Good thing for you I decided to pay this dig of yours a visit and offer an apology to your father."

Thank you, Lord! Anna silently prayed. She knew it was a direct answer to Christian's earlier prayer for help.

Even before Christian and Anna were settled in the boat, the motor roared to life. Bill wasn't kidding when he assured them of his knowledge of the river.

Heading upstream, the old flat-bottomed boat skimmed across the surface with Anna and Christian holding on tightly. Bill skillfully avoided the shallow, grass-clogged areas. Arriving at the campground's boat dock, they positively identified Harry's motorboat moored to one of the posts. Too impatient for the boat to come to a complete stop, Christian leaped onto the landing and swiftly secured the boat to a piling. Looking up, he glimpsed Harry's old yellow pickup truck rounding the corner and speeding out of sight.

"What are we going to do now?" Christian asked in defeat as he stood in the middle of the dirt road leading to the campground. "We don't even have a car."

Running up behind him Anna puffed, "Did you see them?" She glanced behind to see Bill hurriedly following.

"Yeah, I saw them, but we're too late," Christian sighed, shaking his head. *Lord what do we do now?*

"The camp store has a phone; let's call the sheriff's office," Anna suggested.

"Yeah, we don't have any choice!" Christian claimed. "If only we had gotten here a few minutes earlier!"

"What did you expect to do? Charge after Harry who has a gun?" Anna frowned at her brother.

"That's not exactly what I had in mind," Christian answered in defeat.

"We couldn't have stopped him even if we had gotten here earlier." *What I'd like to know is what took them so long to leave?* Anna wondered. "Come-on Christian, we don't have any other choice. Let's call the sheriff."

"We do have a choice!" Christian shouted in elation, pointing to the Suburban® that entered the parking lot. "It's Dad!"

Christian lost no time sprinting toward the vehicle, and Anna sighed with relief while following after him. *Dad will know what to do.*

Dr. Murphy had barely parked when Christian jumped into the front seat and the other two jumped into the back. "Where's the fire?" he jokingly asked.

"Are we glad to see you, Dad!" Anna exclaimed.

"That's apparent," he stated dryly. "And, you must be Bill," Dr. Murphy greeted, turning to shake the older gentleman's hand. "Well then, is there somewhere we're going in a hurry?"

"David was kidnapped!" Anna told her Dad.

"What? I just passed David driving with Harry…" Dr. Murphy's voice trailed off as realization set in. He quickly put the car in reverse.

"Harry kidnapped him!"

"I saw Harry take a right at the main intersection by the Court-house. Maybe we can catch up with them," Dr. Murphy replied tersely. "But we'd better inform the sheriff as well."

Christian attempted to fill his dad in on all that had transpired, pausing only to answer questions Dr. Murphy asked.

"Spanish doubloons! Are you sure?"

"No, but David identified them," Christian answered. "He should know, shouldn't he?"

"I'm uncertain whether or not David could ascertain the authenticity of the coins," Dr. Murphy said. Frowning, he unclipped his phone. "Here Christian, call the sheriff. His number is already programmed."

Christian took the cell phone and scrolled down the numbers until he found the correct one, then hit send. Suddenly his two-way radio sparked to life.

"Turn that off, Son. You must be picking up someone else's signal," Dr. Murphy assessed.

Christian handed the phone over to his father and began to switch his radio off when he heard David's voice. David wasn't talking to them but to Harry! Increasing the volume, Christian held the radio up for all to hear.

"Yes, Sheriff, just a minute, please," Dr. Murphy requested, intrigued to hear David's voice on Christian's two-way radio. They must be close!

"Where are we going?" David questioned.

"None of your business," Harry hissed.

"I might be more cooperative if I knew where you're taking me," David insisted.

The signal wasn't strong and they strained to listen as the words broke up.

"Okay… gonna go to a motel... owes me money. I've…all their dirty work… not gonna hand over the gold! That's why they wanted your father out of the way!"

"My father! What do you know about my father?" David practically shouted.

At that point, there was static interference and they couldn't hear the words.

"I bet the motel he's talking about is the same one we followed Lauren to!" Anna exclaimed.

"It's worth a try," Dr. Murphy said. Speaking into the phone, he quickly relayed as much information as possible about the radio

172

conversation and the motel. "Yes, we'll stay out of the way, but I'm concerned about my nephew. "Yes, sir. 'Bye." He ended the call and clipped the phone to his belt.

The static on the radio continued and Christian lowered the volume. "I guess that's it for now."

"Well," Dr. Murphy informed, "It appears the sheriff's department already suspected Harry of foul play, and they're going to detain Jim at the airport for questioning. Is there no one we can trust?"

Chapter 22

The Confrontation

Sheriff Simons assured them various departments were on top of the case and had already dispatched plain-clothes deputies to the motel. However, Dr. Murphy was not about to be persuaded to simply return to the campground and wait. After convincing the sheriff they would keep out of the way, Dr. Murphy drove toward the motel.

"We can park next-door, like Christian and I did when we followed Lauren," Anna suggested.

Her Dad gave her a sardonic smile. "I never thought I'd appreciate that advice, but it's comforting to know you're familiar with the area."

The radio sputtered once again, and Christian turned it up as the signal grew stronger. "We must be getting closer," he commented as they all listened in.

"Kid, you're gonna stay here while I go and get paid," Harry demanded.

"How are you going to make me?" David angrily responded.

"I'll give you a share of the money I get when I sell the coins."

"Oh, thanks a lot. You're going to pay me off with money that's not even yours. I don't think so," David bit off.

Harry hesitated. "You just stay put, then, and I'll tell you where

175

your old man is."

"So! You do know where my father is!" David shouted, "You've always known and you didn't tell me?"

"Yeah, but if you're not here when I get back, you're not gonna know anything else," Harry threatened.

"Okay, fine. I'll wait for you," David said, defeated, "but if you're not back in five minutes, you're the one who's going to be sorry."

"Yeah, whatever Kid," Harry scoffed, getting out of the truck. He headed to the second floor.

"Hey!" David hissed urgently, "Is anyone there? Christian? Anna? Do you copy?"

Christian jumped when he heard David speaking directly to him. "Hi, David! Yes! We copy!" Christian shouted with elation. "Where are you?"

"It's the same motel you and Anna described. Harry just walked upstairs into some room; I can see it from here."

"We're on the way—not far from there now. Great idea to turn your radio on," Christian enthused, congratulating him.

David laughed. "Yeah, thanks to Uncle Jack who made us keep them on all the time. Good thing Harry was too dumb to remember or notice. How much did you hear?"

Signaling Christian that he wanted the radio, Dr. Murphy asked, "David, are you alright?"

"I'm fine, Uncle Jack."

"We heard most of it, Son. Sheriff Simons should be there. Do you see any patrol cars?"

Quickly surveying the area, David answered in the negative. "No, I don't see anyone except some transients."

"We've just arrived…next door…the white building to your right. Get out of the truck and walk over here," Dr. Murphy directed. He parked the vehicle, alighted, and casually walked over to the same run-down building Christian and Anna had hidden behind. Both teens followed their father, while Bill opted to remain in the vehicle.

"I can't Uncle Jack! Harry knows where they're keeping my dad," he said in elation. "If I'm not here when he gets back, we might

176

never find out where they're keeping him. This is our only chance," David insisted.

"I don't like it, but you've got a point. This is the only lead we have. Just keep your radio on at all times."

I pray we find him quickly, Christian thought. *If they find out Harry has the gold, they may not be so concerned about keeping Uncle Mike alive.* Christian kept his thoughts to himself, not wanting to alarm his cousin.

"Dad, isn't there anything we can do?" Anna pleaded. "I don't see the sheriff anywhere! I thought they said they'd be here."

"We're so close; why don't I sneak upstairs and see if I can eavesdrop on their conversation," Christian suggested. "It looks like a cheap motel with thin walls."

"I think instead of spying, it's time to plead to a higher authority. Let's pray," Dad suggested. "Dear heavenly Father, once again we come before you with our needs. Please watch over David and Mike and keep them safe. Send the authorities quickly and please give us wisdom to know what you want us to do. In Jesus' name we pray, Amen."

"How sad," Anna whispered to Christian once they had finished praying.

"Why do you say that?" Christian asked quietly.

"See those two homeless guys picking through stuff in the dumpsters?"

"Yes, I do," Christian admitted. "But we look worse than they do!"

Anna giggled, despite the circumstances. Looking down at her mud-stained shoes, shorts and shirt, she agreed. "You're right— at least we're dry, but we sure could use a shower!"

"I don't like this. I wish we could get David to safety," Dr. Murphy sighed. He rubbed the back of his neck nervously. Although he had a clear view of the pickup truck and his nephew, Dr. Murphy couldn't see the motel from his vantage point without compromising their position. "I wonder what's taking so long!"

I hope nothing sinister is happening, Anna silently worried. Knowing her father was not normally an impatient man, Anna placed her hand on his arm and said softly, "It'll be okay, Dad. I'm sure Sheriff Simons is on his way." She only prayed that her words would come to pass.

Suddenly a door slammed, and Dr. Murphy signaled for silence. Flattening himself against the building, he looked carefully around the corner. "They're coming!" he whispered.

Christian and Anna were dying to look, but remained flattened against the building at their father's urging. They could see Harry's truck and watched as their cousin sat up from his slouched position. The radio cracked alive. "They're coming... It's some blonde lady, and the guy in the picture you took, Anna...and Harry."

"It must be Lauren and Mr. SUV!" Anna exclaimed.

The group was soon in sight with Harry being held at gunpoint.

"Like I said—do you think I'd have the gold with me?" Harry answered sarcastically.

"Anyone dumb enough to come and get $200 in pay when he has millions in gold in his possession isn't too smart, right Nelson?" Lauren flicked her blonde hair over one shoulder and looked at Nelson for approval.

"So, Mr. SUV's name is Nelson, huh?" Christian asked more to himself.

"Nelson!" Anna whispered, "I wonder if his last name is…"

"Stanley!" Christian finished, looking at Anna in shock. "It couldn't be! The Arcadia mystery!"

This is too much of a coincidence, Anna thought. The Nelson in the article surely must have died long ago.

"Hush you two; listen!" Dr. Murphy directed. Although the building still kept them hidden, the Murphys could now clearly see their cousin and those gathered around him. Holding the two-way radio so they all could listen in, Dr. Murphy put a finger to his lips to signal silence.

"Where's my dad?" David asked to no one in particular.

"What's he doing here?" Lauren asked, dismayed.

"He's my hostage," Harry answered smugly. "See? And y'all call me dumb."

"Yes, Harry, you're very intelligent to add kidnapping to your already long list of offenses," Lauren replied sarcastically.

"Enough of this talk!" Nelson commanded, "Where's the gold?"

"I ain't telling," Harry stammered, "'cause once I do, you're gonna kill me."

"And if you don't give it to me, I'm going to kill you anyway," Nelson threatened with a sinister smirk.

"But—" Harry's words were cut off when in one swift movement Nelson shoved him against the truck and twisted his arm painfully behind his back.

"Hey! You're hurting me!" Harry squealed.

Using his free hand, Nelson quickly frisked Harry's pockets and pulled out a set of keys before throwing him unceremoniously to the ground. "I've had enough of your complaining!" he spat.

"Ahh! You broke my arm!" Harry sat up on the pavement and gingerly rubbed his sore limb.

Nelson forcefully strode to the built-in toolboxes on either side of the truck.

Unlocking the first one, he slammed it down in disgust. "You better not be double-crossing me, Harry!" Nelson warned. Walking to the other side, he unlocked the second toolbox. Reaching inside, he pulled out a canvas bag with one hand.

"It's mine! Stop!" Harry wailed.

"Yours? I think not! After thirty years, my father's treasure has been recovered," he retorted with glee. Pulling the bags out as if they weighed little more than a few pounds each, Nelson set them on the ground beside the truck. Harry remained on the ground, nursing his twisted arm.

"Get out of the truck, Kid! It's time for another ride," Nelson ordered, threatening with his gun once more. "Get up, Harry. You're coming with us."

"We don't need the boy—we have the gold," Lauren suggested as two homeless men approached.

"Anyone got some spare change for food?" one of the men begged.

Nelson yanked Harry in front of him to hide his gun. "Can't you see we're busy?" he snarled. "Go get a real job and earn your money like the rest of us!"

"Sorry," Lauren smiled sweetly, standing in front of David and effectively shielding him. "I didn't bring my purse, and my husband doesn't have his wallet."

The two men sprang into action. One pounced on Nelson, expertly knocking the gun out of his grip. Brandishing his own gun, the transient pointed it at the suspects.

"Okay, Nelson, the gigs over. Hands up! You too, girlfriend." The second plain-clothes deputy pointed his gun toward Lauren indicating she move away from the gold. He then pulled out a radio. Within minutes, sirens sounded and squad cars screeched into the parking lot from all angles. An ambulance and fire trucks arrived close behind. The crooks were soon taken into custody.

The Murphys ran from their hiding place to David's side, while Bill alighted from the car and slowly walked over to join the group.

David sprang out of the truck. "Boy, that was awesome! Did you guys see that?"

"Yes, we saw it," Christian said, slapping his cousin on the shoulder. "Way to go! You did a great job leaving the radio on; that was brilliant!"

David's face was aglow for several seconds before becoming somber at the thought—his dad was still missing. "Hey, where's my dad!" he shouted.

Nelson stood in stony-faced silence. His dark, brooding good looks were marred by a sinister glare. Lauren, while being handcuffed, confessed, "He's okay; he's in room twelve."

David eagerly turned toward the motel, but the sheriff's deputy held up a hand to detain him. "Sir, we need to secure the room before we allow anyone up. There may be more accomplices."

The Murphys waited breathlessly while the sheriff inspected room twelve and adjoining rooms, then signaled for a paramedic to come up. Anna's heart sank. *I hope Uncle Mike's all right!*

Each of the Murphys silently prayed for Mike's safety. Several minutes later, the sheriff signaled they were clear to come up.

Taking two stairs at a time, David was the first to see his father. Dr. Murphy was directly behind. Dressed in hospital scrubs and barefoot, Dr. Mike Murphy looked wonderful for a man who had been near death days earlier.

"Dad! Are you okay?" David asked as he threw himself into his father's arms.

"David! I'm fine, now, son!" Mike responded, hugging David and choking back tears of joy. He shook his brother's hand and then stood to give him a hug.

"Great to see you!" Mike grinned.

"You look incredible!" Jack happily remarked, "Come on—let's get out of here!" Turning to the paramedic who was packing up, he quickly asked, "He can go—can't he?"

"Yes, sir; he's fine," the paramedic smiled at the happy scene. "Normally standard procedure is to transport him to the hospital for a complete physical and some fluids if needed, but his vital signs are normal. Besides, I think he's been through enough for one day."

"If needed, I'll have my brother bring me later, if you don't mind," Mike informed.

Walking down the rickety stairs, the Murphys observed the parking lot still lit up like a Christmas tree. "Sheriff, are we free to go?" Jack Murphy asked.

"Not yet. I have a few questions to ask Mike," Sheriff Simons ordered.

Anna looked nervously over her shoulder where Nelson and Lauren sat in the back of two separate sheriff's cars. "You know, it's too bad Lauren is married to Nelson. I really liked her," she whispered to Christian. "It's too bad she's mixed up in all of this—there's too much damaging evidence against her."

"Yeah," Christian agreed. "Hey, isn't that Agent Spencer?" Christian observed, nudging Anna with his elbow. He motioned with his head toward one of the undercover deputies dressed as a homeless person.

"You're right, but I barely recognized him with all that facial hair and no FBI gear!" Anna exclaimed. "Boy, I wish I had my camera right now!"

At that, David and Christian burst out laughing. Mike stood with his arm around David's shoulder, looking quizzically at the boys. "What's so funny?"

They all watched as one of the sheriff's deputies drove off with a dejected and scowling Nelson in custody. As soon as most of the emergency vehicles pulled away, Agent Spencer walked to the car where Lauren waited and removed her handcuffs. The Murphys watched in stunned silence.

"Thanks," Lauren smiled, rubbing her wrists. She accepted Agent Spencer's hand as he helped her out of the car, and they walked to where the startled Murphys stood.

"Remember kids, crime doesn't pay," Tyler Spencer reminded. He winked while peeling off the tattered, oversized flannel shirt, revealing his white, sweat-stained tank top underneath.

"Tyler and Lauren, right?" Christian asked.

"Yes; that's correct. Since we realized you recognized us, we thought it would be best to clarify some things," Tyler explained.

"Actually my name is Sarah, not Lauren. I'm not married to Nelson. I'm an undercover agent for the FBI, and you already know that Tyler works for the agency as well."

Christian and Anna exchanged looks. Their initial hunch that Lauren couldn't possibly be criminally involved had been correct. Perhaps they were better at this detective stuff than they thought!

"You can imagine our surprise at seeing you Murphys here," Sarah laughed. It was just too much of a coincidence. First in the Keys, then here!

"We didn't realize the connection to your uncle until later, so we actually suspected you were involved, too," Tyler added.

"Is that why you avoided us at the campground, Sarah?" Anna asked.

"Yes, I was returning from spying on the excavation with Nelson when you arrived at the campground. And," Sarah added, "you were the last people I expected to see in Arcadia! I also know you followed me to the motel the other day."

"And we thought we had done all of that unobserved!" Christian laughed. "Guess we need to work on our undercover tactics, Anna."

"Actually, your sharp observation is what worried Sarah. She was afraid you would get too close and call the sheriff, which would have ruined everything we were trying to do. Especially since you probably heard the scream coming from the room," Tyler replied.

"Oh, yes, what was that all about?" Anna asked.

"Um," Sarah admitted embarrassed, "I had to deck Nelson."

Smiling, Tyler put a protective arm around Sarah. "That's my wife; she can take care of herself."

What? Sarah is married to Tyler? Man, were we off base, Anna mused to herself, smiling widely.

"Well," Sarah continued, "we decided to contact Sheriff Simons before you did, and he was more than willing to cooperate with us."

"What case were you working on, and how did we get involved?" Mike asked.

"It's a bit complicated," Sarah explained.

"I think I've caught up on my rest for the next few years. What were you giving me? Sleeping pills?"

"Yes, but I halved the dose," Sarah said. "Actually Harry purchased them and insisted we keep you sedated. Nelson and I met him one day at the drugstore. He wanted you out of the way. He believed if you were gone the dig would fold."

"I thought Harry worked for Nelson. How did he have a say in how you ran your operation?" David asked. He couldn't imagine anyone listening to anything Harry had to say.

"Actually they were working together," Tyler replied, holding up his hand to stifle the ensuing objections. "I know, it doesn't seem probable, but it's a long story."

Sarah added, "With Nelson being trigger-happy and thinking of you as an inconvenience, the idea to sedate you was a good and temporary solution."

"But why would Nelson want to kidnap Uncle Mike, anyway?"

"I think we'd better start at the beginning," Tyler suggested.

"You'll be needing the rest of the gold, won't you?"

David clarified.

"What do you mean?" Tyler quizzed, "Isn't this all the gold?"

"Harry had me hide some for safe keeping before we left the campground," David smiled. "Apparently he didn't trust Nelson to split it with him."

"So that's what took you so long that we almost caught up with you," Christian shook his head. "No wonder!"

"Well, it appears we will need to retrieve the remainder of the gold. Can you direct us to its whereabouts, David?" Tyler asked.

"Yes; it's at the campground. Harry decided to hide it near Uncle Jack's trailer!"

"Excuse me," Sheriff Simons, a heavyset man interrupted. "Dr. Jack Murphy?"

"Yes?"

"We weren't able to detain Jim Johnson at the local airstrip; the private plane left before we could speak with him. Where is his final destination?"

"A lab in Texas," Dr. Murphy informed. "I'd be happy to provide you with the lab's phone number and Jim's cell phone number as well."

"We'll have the authorities in Texas contact him for us." The sheriff nodded and walked away.

"Tell you what—it looks like you need to clean up, and so do we. Why don't we meet after dinner? How does 7 o'clock at the campground sound?" Tyler suggested. "We can pick up the remainder of the gold and debrief you all at the same time."

"It's a deal," Dr. Murphy responded, speaking for them all.

As the elated group headed for the car, Mike announced, "And no one eats until they first shower! What have you all been into? You should see yourselves!"

The Murphys dissolved into laughter and each tried to fill Mike in on various details.

"Arcadia Man's headed to Texas, Dad!"

"It poured!"

"He fell from the helicopter."

"Jim was almost killed!"

"Enough!" Mike shouted, holding up his hands to stifle the flow of information. "As much as I'm dying to find out, let's first get showered and fed back at the campsite. Then I'll be ready to take in all the details."

*Now this is the way a rescue should b*e, Anna thought happily as they were en route to the campground.

Chapter 23

The Truth Will Set You Free

After a brief stop for groceries on the way back to the campground, Bill, an excellent cook, prepared dinner while the others cleaned up. Food had never tasted so good! As the group ate, they compared notes.

"You see," Bill remarked with a forkful of potato salad in midair, "Nelson Stanley was who the sheriff ran off thirty years ago. And we know it can't be the same fellow, 'cause this one is too young."

"Could it be a relative? A son perhaps?" Christian asked.

"Well, now you could have something there," Bill replied, munching on the salad.

"To tell you the truth," he laughed, "I tried the same antics with them folks as I did with you. Took some tools out of their shed and tried to make them leave."

"We didn't see a shed," Anna reminded him.

"No, it was destroyed in a storm and torn down long ago," Bill explained.

"Didn't someone live on that property? And didn't they notice strange activities in their own back yard?" David asked.

"An older couple by the name of Robinson, I believe, lived there at the time. They were too busy traveling to notice anyone using their boathouse. Besides, it was almost a half a mile to the river. They never ventured that far back."

"No wonder! A perfect place for smugglers to bring their loot! But why bother burying it?" Mike asked.

"That I don't know. Rumor has it that there were two partners, and one double-crossed the other. Nelson Stanley, the older one, somehow acquired illegal valuables and was waiting for a buyer—but the deal fell through. Why he came to the southwest coast and our small town remains a mystery."

The dishes were barely cleared before the two FBI agents drove up in a plain brown four-door sedan.

"What, no Range Rover® ?" Christian teased, as Sarah and Tyler alighted.

"No, the FBI budget doesn't allow for luxury SUV's," Sarah laughed. "Besides, it belonged to Nelson and was confiscated by the sheriff's department.

"Do you have the gold?" Tyler asked.

"Yes, we moved the sack to the back of my car," Dr. Murphy replied as he and Tyler walked over to unlock the vehicle.

"Looks like he kept the majority of the gold in here! That not-so-smart man, was smarter than we thought!" Tyler exclaimed, laughing.

Several picnic tables had been placed together and the group sat down to enjoy the evening air. "Can we offer you something to eat or drink? Lemonade?" Anna asked.

"Thanks. We already ate, but lemonade sounds good." The agents accepted the cold drink and sat down next to Christian who had moved over to make room on the bench.

"It's debriefing time," Sarah began. "I'm sure you understand the importance of keeping the information you happened upon private. We'd like to relate some of the recent events and ascertain if there is any information you can add."

The Murphys nodded their heads.

"Let's start at the beginning of your involvement," Sarah began. Launching into an explanation, she gave a brief overview of a ring of artifact smugglers. "We received a tip that the captain of the Wahoo

Racer was carrying contraband back and forth. He would take a group of fishermen out, sometimes under the pretense of a free trip. While at sea, he would pull up crab traps containing gold or artifacts that had been placed there by a well-organized ring of smugglers. Captain Slate was a middle-man."

"But why a free trip?" Dr. Murphy asked.

"Actually, it was brilliant," Sarah remarked. "You see, the passengers wouldn't be expecting much. If you had paid for the trip, you'd want better service—baiting your fish, taking it off—that sort of thing. Did you notice how Slate barely lifted a finger?"

"No, not really. We were having too much fun!" Christian confessed.

"Exactly, and that's what he counted on," Tyler commented.

"Well, while you were busy catching fish, he was busy pulling up crab traps."

"Yes, I did notice him doing that," Anna said. "I think I took a picture of it."

"Well, you and I were probably the only ones who saw him. I wasn't able to see what he pulled in, and when the authorities searched the boat later on, nothing suspicious was found."

"How did we get involved in the chase?" Dr. Murphy asked.

"That was awesome!" Christian exclaimed. "I'll never forget it!"

"An experience I personally would like to forget," Dr. Murphy added, sardonically. Everyone laughed, and Dr. Murphy smiled good-naturedly.

"Actually, it was a set up," Tyler filled in. "Slate's boat was a decoy for the one we ended up chasing! The other boat was picking up a package left in a crab trap when they received a warning that agents were on their trail. So, they sent Slate out to lure our attention away from them."

"Didn't you know you had the wrong boat?" Christian asked. "Wasn't Sarah undercover?"

"I didn't know Slate had planned to invite your family," Sarah clarified. "I was trying to catch Slate in the act of retrieving the stolen contraband from the traps."

"We didn't realize we had the wrong boat until we saw your family onboard," Tyler ruefully remembered.

"But Lauren, I mean Sarah," Anna said, giggling as she corrected herself. "We saw the other boat blow up! Yet, in the pictures I took, Nelson Stanley was on the other boat before it was destroyed. How did he survive?"

"You took pictures of Nelson on the other boat?" Sarah asked in amazement. "We could enter those as evidence! May we have the film, please?" Sarah and Tyler looked at each other in surprise, while Dr. Murphy proudly beamed at his daughter.

"Great agents we are," Tyler said, laughing. "We didn't notice you taking pictures. It's probably a good thing we didn't, or we would have confiscated your film."

Anna smiled at Christian who winked back at her. He was glad he had advised Anna to hide her camera.

"That still doesn't explain the boat exploding!" Christian reminded them.

Sighing, Tyler explained, "Well it's embarrassing, but they got away. Our divers found no signs of human remains that might have been visible had the perpetrators died in the explosion. Do you remember seeing all those dive boats with 'divers down' flags?"

"Yes, it was lobster season and many of the boats had red flags with a white diagonal slash through the middle," Dr. Murphy remembered.

"Well, our talented crooks put on scuba equipment, took their stash, and jumped overboard before blowing up their boat by remote signal. They led us to believe they had died in the explosion," Tyler explained.

"And they would have fooled us, if I hadn't been Slate's first mate," Sarah confirmed. "You see, Nelson asked Slate to accompany him to Arcadia to retrieve the gold. Slate didn't want to leave, so he sent me instead. You can imagine my surprise at seeing Nelson. We suspected he was part of the ring, but we didn't know the extent of his involvement and weren't positive he was onboard the other boat—until now!"

"Sarah, how did you get to be a first mate, if you don't mind me asking?" Dr. Murphy wanted to know.

"I grew up on the Florida Keys and my father owned his own charter company. He was a captain until he retired. I practically grew up on boats. You see, I'm one of the locals," Sarah smiled. "I just neglected to inform people about what I studied while in college," she added.

"But, why Arcadia? And how did Nelson know there was gold buried here?" Bill asked, quietly taking it all in.

"This crime ring goes back approximately forty years. They steal from other crooks and don't even have a good reputation around their own kind. The Spanish doubloons were stolen from an excavating crew that salvaged a wreck in the Keys. The gold was to go to a museum, but it never arrived. Nelson Stanley, Sr. and his partner managed to intercept the valuables, but couldn't agree on how they would divide the profit once they found a buyer for it. Therefore, Nelson decided to outwit his partner. Instead of going to his known hideouts in the Keys or Miami, he settled upon an obscure location on the southwest coast. The person who gave him the idea was Allard Bradley, a local Arcadian who worked part time on the fishing boats in the Keys."

"But Nelson Stanley doesn't look—what—sixty or so years old," Jack remarked.

"No, our Nelson is Nelson Stanley, Jr.," Tyler supplied.

"So why was he coming back after all these years to retrieve the gold?" Mike asked.

"Because he just found out the note his father left him was authentic!" Sarah informed. "Let me explain. In a bizarre set of circumstances, it appears history was repeating itself. Nelson Sr. decided to bury the gold for safekeeping, but it appears the man who was digging the hole to bury it was electrocuted and died. Apparently he fell on a power line—or one fell on him; we're not sure. There was no way Nelson could help him without getting electrocuted himself, and if he called for help, his gold would be discovered. So Nelson just piled as much dirt as he could over the top of the man and buried him with the gold, figuring he was already dead."

"We never completely understood why Nelson left a sizeable

191

trail connecting him to many illegal dealings," Tyler initiated. "We surmise it was due to the storm—actually, a hurricane—which would explain why he was in such a hurry to leave. The authorities uncovered information linking him to many unsolved mysteries. Nelson never returned to retrieve the gold; it was as if he had disappeared. We now know that he died while on his way back home, but not before mailing a note to his son telling about the treasure and the sudden death of the man who buried it. Since Nelson Jr. was only two at the time, his mother saved the note for him. She considered it an exaggerated tale, and when Nelson grew up and received the note, he disregarded it, thinking it fictitious. The only other person who knew of the gold's whereabouts was the man who buried it, and he was also dead."

"Who was it that died at the river?" Bill asked. "It wasn't Allard, was it?"

"Yes, we believe it was," Sarah replied.

"Well now, that explains it," Bill stated. "I knew Allard. Grew up with him and he was always up to no good. I had seen him in town before the storm, but no one ever saw him afterwards. When the hurricane blew through here, many power lines came down. A month or two after returning home, the Robinsons received an enormous electric bill. That was the first time they realized someone had been using electricity in the shed. Calling the power company to have the electricity turned off, they never considered looking for buried gold, as they had no idea what the thieves had be up to. The sheriff and his men, however, did uncover evidence against Nelson Stanley at the time."

"But that still doesn't explain how Nelson Jr. discovered the note was authentic," David remarked.

"Harry was Allard's son," Sarah explained. "He followed in his father's footsteps and worked on fishing boats in the Keys. Hearing rumors about Nelson and gold buried in Arcadia, Harry remembered stories relating to his own father's death. Slowly he put the pieces together. Meeting Nelson and hearing him discuss his father was all Harry needed. Remembering his dad had worked for a man named Nelson Stanley, he felt it was more than a coincidence. When he told Nelson Jr., they realized the note might have some validity to it and was worth a try."

"Why didn't Harry just dig up the gold himself?"

"He didn't know exactly where in Arcadia, but Nelson did. Nelson promised to pay Harry to help dig for the gold."

"But that still doesn't explain why they kidnapped me," Mike said.

"They needed you out of the way. They weren't planning on finding an anthropological dig right where they were expecting to find gold!"

"So, if Uncle Mike were out of the way, they thought the dig would fold?" Christian asked for clarification.

"Yes, but they didn't count on the tenacity of Jim!" Mike said, laughing.

"You're right," Sarah picked up. "So Harry decided to hurry things along. He even slit the tents after Bill tried his hand at scaring you off the dig site. He figured Bill would be blamed, so no one would suspect him."

"Sorry folks," Bill piped in sheepishly.

"It's okay, Bill. We know why you did it, and you weren't the malicious one," Anna acknowledged.

"So," Mike summarized out loud, "What we actually excavated was Allard?"

"Yes, we believe so, but we don't have any proof," Sarah answered.

"But that skeleton would only have been buried for thirty years, not thirty million years!" David exclaimed. "The age dating proved the fossil is ancient!"

"Just a minute," Anna said while jumping up. She hastily went to the camper and came back. "I found this in the specimen tent and put it in my pocket accidentally. I almost forgot I had it!" She handed it over to her uncle.

"You removed something from the specimen tent? Bad girl," David teased, smiling.

"Yeah, well, it was when you guys found the box and Christian was yelling to bring shovels," Anna explained in her own defense. "I stuck it in my pocket without thinking."

Mike took the baggie and looked at the outer markings. "By this location, it was found near the upper torso of Arcadia Man." Mike used the baggie to hold the rock while he inverted it, making sure not to touch it with his hands. "If I touch this rock, the residue from my hands could throw off the age dating results," he explained to the puzzled agents.

"Well, look at this!" Mike smiled, first showing his brother.

Jack grinned and reached out to touch the rock. "So! The 'missing link' is still missing," he laughed in elation.

"But I thought you said—" Sarah began.

"What did you find?" David asked.

"Here is your proof," Jack answered, chuckling as he handed the coin to the startled agent. "It's a 1967 penny imbedded in fossilized rock, which would put the fossil to say, around what—thirty or so years old?"

"Give or take some years," Mike added, laughing good-naturedly.

"What? The fossil we excavated really isn't the missing link?" David asked.

"No, Son, I'm afraid not. I think this penny links our fossil to Allard, a man who lived in Arcadia. I had suspected that Jim was hiding some evidence, but never thought it was this! That's why I wanted Jack here and my urgency in wanting him to know I thought the fossil might be younger than our earlier predictions. I didn't want the media to get wind of a missing link, unless it could be substantiated."

"But, how could it become fossilized so quickly?" David asked, still trying to assimilate all the information.

"This area contains phosphate which hastens the fossilization process, even if we are not exactly sure how it happens," Jack replied, looking at Mike for confirmation. "It appears that if what was said here tonight is true…"

Mike interrupted his brother, adding, "We can only guess, but Allard was electrocuted over a long period of time, then buried in sandy limestone, perhaps with phosphate. I'm sure the river levels have risen and fallen through the years. And, having been buried for over thirty years…"

"Could very possibly cause the flesh to become fossilized," Jack continued his brother's train of thought, "and then the fact that he was completely buried, quickly, allowed him to become preserved rather than decay."

Mike shook his head in agreement. "A similar phenomenon happened when tree roots were fossilized in moments when a high voltage line fell near Grand Prairie, in Alberta, Canada in 1973. When scientists were asked what the results would be if these specimens were dated by ^{14}C, they said the tests would be meaningless because they would indicate an age of millions of years due to an intervening heat process being involved," he explained.

"So that's what threw off the ^{14}C dating, Dad? Heat from the electrocution?" David inquired for clarification.

"Yes, I'm afraid so," Mike answered. "This is obviously not the missing link."

Christian began smiling and looked at Anna to see if she was following his train of thought, then looked at David and began chuckling.

"Is Jim ever going to be surprised when he finds out!" Anna said aloud, guessing what her brother had been thinking.

David looked at his cousins and began laughing. It was contagious, and soon the three of them were roaring. The surprised adults looked on. When David was able to talk, he filled his father in on Jim's obsession with fame and his belief the discovery would gain him status in the anthropological world.

"Apparently several magazines offered Jim in excess of a hundred thousand dollars each for interviews," Jack informed. "One museum offered him a million dollars for exclusive rights. I just found this out when we were inundated with reporters at the airport. That's why he was in such a hurry to get Arcadia Man excavated. He had a deadline and money to make." Dr. Murphy looked at his brother and stated, "My greatest concern in being involved with this excavation was that you were trying to make a case for evolution."

"I never set out to prove or disprove Creationism, or to get rich," Mike reassured, looking at his brother to confirm that Jack

195

understood his goals were not similar to Jim's. "I just uncover the facts and chart them. We do our best to estimate the age of each artifact given the limited tools we have on hand. I wish we had perfect age-dating techniques at our disposal, but we don't. Even Potassium Argon, K-Ar dating has its flaws."

"I know you're honest," Jack said, then added quietly, "but sometimes a scientist's preconceived notion can color his outlook— such as with Jim. He obviously found this coin. Since no one else had seen it, he chose not to share this information with any of us."

"We're just lucky he didn't destroy it," Christian said.

"He wasn't expecting us to pack up for him," David reminded them. "He normally would have been in charge of sorting through all fossils to form a relative chronology when we got back. After his close call with the helicopter, he wasn't thinking too clearly and obviously forgot all about it."

"So, he never expected us to find it?" Anna asked.

"Well, although that's not very honest, it's not exactly a crime in the FBI world," Sarah said while standing. "If you have the film, Anna, we'll be getting back. We need to leave first thing in the morning."

Anna hurried to the camper to get the negatives, glad her photographs were useful after all!

Later, after their guests had left, the Murphys sat around a campfire similar to the one they had made when Uncle Mike had been sick.

"So," Anna asked, "Jim didn't have anything to do with you getting sick?"

"No, Anna, I just contracted the flu and it turned into pneumonia. Jim's only crime, I'm afraid, was trying to make this fossil fit into his preconceived notions and personal agenda."

"Well, all that leaves is *Archaeoraptor*," Jack said, "the dinosaur-to-bird link."

"*Archaeoraptor*?" Mike repeated, smiling. "That fraud?"

"What!"

"Yes, the supposedly 125-million year old specimen is

actually two different creatures put together. It initially escaped detection by a team of scientists and top experts on bird origins—that is, until they examined the site of origin in China. They grew suspicious the dinosaur-like tail might not belong to the rest of the animal. Upon visiting a fossil dealer, the team found a different dinosaur with a tail that matched the tail on the bird specimen."

"So they combined the head of a birdlike creature with a dinosaur's tail?" Christian clarified.

"Yes, that's right."

"How did you know this?" Jack asked, looking stunned. "I suspected it couldn't be true, but I was floored when I read the article in a popular scientific magazine, especially in the context of what we were excavating."

"I read about *Archaeoraptor* in one of the publications I received. Actually, I believe it was in an open letter to Dr. Peter Raven, the Secretary for research and exploration of the National Geographic Society. The letter was from Storrs Olson, curator of birds at the Smithsonian Institute's Museum of Natural History. In his letter, he openly criticized the *National Geographic* for engaging in sensationalistic and unsubstantiated journalism.

"Really? How did I miss that?" Jack stated.

Laughing, Mike remarked, "I think it's a good idea you decided to give up archaeology and take up photography!"

"I couldn't agree with you more," Jack admitted.

"Wow! I still can't believe we actually helped solve not just one, but two mysteries," Anna observed.

Christian beamed, "Yeah, it was really great."

David looked up and smiled with amazement. "Life sure isn't boring with you guys around. I think we need to visit more often."

A look of agreement crossed everyone's faces; they looked forward to spending more time together.

"So, Uncle Mike," Christian ventured, "when's the next excavation scheduled for?"

Dr. Murphy and Anna shook their heads and laughed in unison, "No more digging!"

Epilogue

The Murphys were gathered around a hospital bed. This time it was a joyous occasion. They had returned home two days earlier, just in time. Their mother went into labor two weeks prematurely. The siblings vied to hold Julie Anne Murphy and Michael David Murphy.

"Its my turn to hold her."

"Okay. Trade you Julie for Michael," Anna said.

"What about me?" Andy interrupted.

Kathy and Jack clasped hands and watched as all five of their children, happily squabbled.

"Hi, everyone!" Came a cheerful, voice from the door.

"I'm so glad you're here!" exclaimed Kathy, smiling.

"David and I knew we couldn't be this close and not come to visit," Mike said with a grin, holding an unbelievably large bouquet of flowers, "especially with such an exciting event taking place. And twins, no less!"

David looked from one baby to the other saying, "They look exactly alike!"

Everyone burst into laughter and Christian and Anna exchanged smiles, they were going to enjoy not only the brand-new additions to the family, but the ones that had been lost, and now were found.

Letter From the Editor:

Dear Readers,

While the characters and the plot within these pages are fictitious, there are many scientific facts that are true.

The Murphy family and all the characters, the Science Museum and the events of finding the gold and Arcadia Man are all fictional. The places, however, do exist. Although the Arcadia campground is a real place, as is the Peace River, the events happening there are fictitious.

Everything to do with carbon dating, evolution, and Creation Science is true and can be found in resources provided by leading Creation Science centers. We tried to portray those who believe in Evolution and those who believe in Creation in a truthful manner. Stating both viewpoints help to make the positions understood.

In real life there is much discussion and disagreement on this issue, often causing tempers to flare. Each should learn what the other believes and attempt to make inroads into finding a common ground so truth may be known on all accounts. While the writers of this book are believers of the Biblical account of Creation, our focus was not to put one group down by elevating another. We feel the facts speak for themselves. Facts supporting Creation are overwhelming although only a few examples are mentioned in this book.

The only aspect of this book relating to science that is pure fiction is the fossilized Arcadia Man. There is no scientific evidence that we are aware of that would substantiate the fossilization of a man in the way we describe. While it is true that extreme heat can throw off Carbon 14 dating, we have no proof other than our imaginations that a constant high electrical voltage would turn a body into fossilized remains. The other scientific events discussed in this novel can be found in leading Creation Science books and magazines and are all factual.

All of the articles we spoke about are true. *Archaeoraptor* was indeed written about in the *National Geographic*, and the Smithsonian curator of Birds, Storrs Olson, did write an open letter about this "find" in an article.

It is our prayer that through reading this novel you have become aware of scientific support in the study of origins. Understandably, some of the scientific terminology can be difficult; that is why we provided a glossary for you in the back of this book. Remember when studying that no matter what the field, keep your eyes focused on Him—for the Truth will indeed set you free!

About the Authors

Christina Gerwitz was 17 when she completed writing this book. She is a homeschool graduate and learned her love of writing at an early age. Majoring in Communications with a minor in Anthropology, Christina plans to graduate from Florida Gulf Coast University in the spring of 2004. She has an advanced certification in SCUBA and enjoys sports, teaching children of all ages at church, reading, watching movies, and being with her family and friends. You may email her at Writer4JMJ@aol.com.

Felice Gerwitz, along with her husband and best friend, Jeffrey, own Media Angels,® Inc., a publishing company dedicated to producing quality materials for parents. Having dreamed of writing a novel but not motivated to do so alone, Felice credits her daughter's contributions of plot development and persistent encouragement to the success of this finished product.

Involved in homeschooling since 1986, Felice and Jeffrey graduated two of their children, Neal and Christina, and Felice continues to school Nicholas, Anne, and Michael. Felice is thankful for her husband who is both supportive of her writing and a wonderful spiritual influence in her life. You may contact Felice either by e-mail at MediaAngels@aol.com, or through her website, www.MediaAngels.com, which contains more titles she has written.

Acknowledgments

The authors would like to thank the following people, for without their help this book wouldn't be possible:

Thank you, Frank Sherwin, Tom DeRosa, and Jill Whitlock, for your expertise in the area of Creation Science. Jan Sherwin, thank you for discussing Carbon 14 dating with Dr. Andrew Snelling from ICR, and we thank you, Dr. Snelling, for so graciously giving of your time.

To our family who listened to countless readings, Neal, and Jeff, we give our undying gratitude. Gabriela Martinez, Viktorija and Kristina Krulikas, Megan Hogmire, and Cathy Farnham, you are special friends. Taking the time to read the manuscript was a special blessing to us. Thanks. And to grandma Margaret Ann Gerwitz, we give you an extra special thanks and hug.

To our editors, Jan Sherwin and Jackie Perseghetti, you ladies make us look good! Thank you for your tireless work.

Glossary

As culled from Merriam-Webster's Collegiate Dictionary 2002 CD-Rom unless otherwise specified.

Anthropology: Science dealing with the study of humans in relation to distribution, origin, classification, relationship of races, physical character, environmental and social relations, and culture.

Archaeology: The study of ancient civilizations to determine something about the culture through excavation, identification, through the study of remains such as graves, buildings, tools and pottery.

Archaeologist: Scientists who study the lives of early people and analyze the objects those people left behind.

Arm-to-leg ratio: The relationship in degree or number between two similar things.

Bow: The front part of a boat or ship.

Carbon-14: Carbon 14 age dating (Also known as ^{14}C). This method, discovered by Williard Libby in 1947, is used to measure the amount of low-level ^{14}C remaining in dead organic matter. The results enable scientists to calculate how long ago a plant or animal died. The dates are only approximate and many things can cause it to fluctuate.

Chronology: The science that deals with the dating and sequence of events.

Creation: An act by God, the Divine Creator, which brought the world into existence.

Evolution: The false belief that new types of organisms descend from earlier ones over great amounts of times, such as a bird descending from a dinosaur. The belief in evolution requires an increase in genetic information and the ability of the organism to pass on new traits to their offspring. This has never been demonstrated. This is not to be confused with microevolution which is a term used for small changes that can be readily observed, such as various breeds of cats. Macroevolution implies large changes such as sea creatures evolving into dogs. The latter is the belief that Darwin made popular. (Definition gathered from information presented by the Institute for Creation Research.)

Excavation site: An area that is carefully dug and documented in order to learn about a civilization that lived long ago.

Femur: A bone of the leg found between the pelvis and knee in humans. The largest and strongest bone in the body, it is also called the thighbone.

Fossilization: The formation of impressions and carbonization that happens when decaying tissue leaves behind traces of carbon and mineral reactions, or changes. Fossilization can simply be described as hardened remains.

Fossils: The remains of an organism of the past, such as a skeleton or leaf imprint, that is embedded and preserved in the earth's crust.

Geologic column: A suggested arrangement of the major earth layers into an order considered "perfect" by many secular scientists.

Half-life: The time it takes for the radioactivity of material taken in by a living organism to be reduced to half its initial value by both biological processes and radioactive decay. (This applies to ^{14}C.)

Hoax: Something that has been accepted by fraudulent means.

Homo erectus: An extinct species of human beings regarded

as an ancestor of Homo sapiens.

Homo sapien: The modern species of human beings.

Juvenile: Not fully-grown or developed; young.

Leaching: When water passes through a fossil and takes away part of the material, such as mineral in bone.

Mastodon: A very large, extinct mammal that resembles the elephant.

Misrepresentation: To give incorrect or misleading facts; to be dishonest or lead someone into believing something other than the truth.

Neanderthal Man: Some evolutionists label it an extinct species or race of human beings, *Homo Neanderthalensis*, that supposedly lived during the late Pleistocene Age in the Old World. Creationists believe *Neanderthal* man was fully human.

Paleoanthropologist: A scientist who studies the remains and fossils of ancient man.

Paleontologist: A scientist who studies the remains of animals, plants, and other organisms that lived long ago.

Petrifaction: This happens when plants and animals become fossilized after mineral rich water soaks into the pores of the original hard parts, solidifying and preserving it.

Pilt-down Man: A supposed early human species constructed from a skull allegedly found in a gravel bed around 1912. However, in 1953, it was determined to be a fake, constructed from a human cranium and the jawbone of an ape.

Port: The left-hand side of a ship or aircraft facing forward.

Prehistoric: The time before language was first recorded in writing.

Preservation: To keep something from decaying or decomposing.

Radioactive dating: An inexact dating method. Radioactive isotopes are forms of chemical elements that break down or decay to form other materials. Although scientists know approximate rates of decay for various radioactive isotopes, many factors may affect the results.

Shallow water invertebrate: An animal, such as an insect or a shellfish, which lacks a backbone or spinal column.

Site chronology: A blend of various dating methods used on things that have been found, to establish the order in which something occurred naturally in time. The scientist creates a chart of the order of layers of the earth and from this develops a relationship between the things found on the site, according to where they were found.

Starboard: The right-hand side of a ship if you face forward.

Stern: The rear end of a boat or ship.

Stratum: A layer. Two or more layers are called "strata."

SUV: Acronym for sports-utility vehicle

Transitional forms: An organism that seems to be turning into something else; an in-between or intermediate stage of an organism.

Unstable: Decaying within a relatively short lifetime.

References:

Bliss, Richard, et al. Fossils: Key to the Present. Santee, CA: Institute for Creation Research, 1980.

Cuozzo, Jack. Buried Alive, The Startling Truth About Neanderthal Man. Green Forest, AZ: Master Books, 1998.

DeRosa, Tom. Fossils in Florida. Audiotape. FPEA Convention, Orlando, FL: recorded by Magnemedia, Inc., 1999.

Gerwitz, Felice and Jill Whitlock. Creation Astronomy: A Study Guide to the Constellations. Ft. Myers, FL: Media Angels, Inc., 1995.

Gerwitz, Felice and Jill Whitlock. Creation Geology: A Study Guide to Fossils, Formations and The Flood. Ft. Myers, FL: Media Angels, Inc., 1997.

Gerwitz, Felice and Jill Whitlock. Creation Science: A Study Guide to Creation. Ft. Myers, FL: Media Angels, Inc., 2003.

Lubenow, Marvin. Bones of Contention A Creationist Assessment of Human Fossils. Grand Rapids, MI: Master Books, 1992.

Mayell, Hillary, "Feathered Dino Fossils Prompt New Look at Ancient Cultures." National Geographic. 20 Sept 2000. [www.NationalGeographic.com].

Moffet, Barbara, "Archaeoraptor Statement." National Geographic. 21 Jan 2000. [www.NationalGeographic.com].

Olson, Storrs. Open Letter To: Dr. Peter Raven, Secretary Committee for Research and Exploration, National Geographic Society. National Museum of Natural History, Smithsonian Institution. Reprinted: Answers in Genesis Ministries International, 2000.

Petersen, Dennis. Unlocking the Mysteries of Creation. El Dorado, CA: Creation Resource Foundation, 1990.

Press Release, "Dino-Bird Controversy." National Geographic. 21 Jan 2000. [www.NationalGeographic.com].

Richards, Lawrence. It Couldn't Just Happen. Dallas, TX: Word Publishing, Inc., 1989.

Tejada, Susan. "Dinosaurs Raise a Flap." National Geographic. 15 Oct 1999. [www.NationalGeographic.com].

Tejada, Susan. "Dinosaurs Are Not Extinct: Their Descendants Fill The Sky." National Geographic. 15 Oct 1999. [www.NationalGeographic.com].

Resources:

Creation Studies Institute (Mr. Tom DeRosa)
2401 West Cypress Creek Rd.
Ft. Lauderdale, FL 33309
[www.csinfo.org]

Institute for Creation Research (Dr. John Morris)
PO Box 1606
El Cajon, CA 92022
(619) 448-0900
[www.icr.org]

Answers in Genesis (Mr. Ken Ham)
PO Box 6330
Florence, KY 41022
(606) 727-2222
[www.answersingenesis.org]

Media Angels,® Inc. (Mrs. Felice Gerwitz)
[www.MediaAngels.com]
Website includes numerous creation-research links
and online newsletter. Media Angels publishes curriculum
for parents and educators. Email for a free catalog.